• • •

A STRONG SURGE YANKED ME OFF THE GROUND AND I HELD on with every ounce of strength I had left. I yelled in frustration, and soon realized I wasn't the only one yelling. A body flew past me. Someone had lost their battle with the storm. I craned my neck and watched as the body was flung higher and higher into the air, like a ragdoll. It must have been fifty feet in the air when it got caught in the wind shear. The wind slammed it straight into the cactus grove. Several sharp spines drove clear through the body, pinning it hallway up the cactus. It didn't move, and I guessed it wasn't going to.

Still clinging to the rock, my only thought was a selfish one.

The odds just got a little better.

ALSO BY KRISTI HELVIG
Strange Skies

• • •

OTHER EGMONT USA BOOKS
YOU MIGHT ENJOY

BZRK
by Michael Grant

Human.4
by Mike A. Lancaster

Quarantine, Book 1: The Loners
by Lex Thomas

Tabula Rasa
by Kristen Lippert-Martin

KRISTI HELVIG

BURN OUT

EGMONT
Publishing
NEW YORK

EGMONT
We bring stories to life

First published in the United States by Egmont Publishing, 2014
This paperback edition published by Egmont Publishing, 2015
443 Park Avenue South, Suite 806
New York, NY 10016

1 3 5 7 9 8 6 4 2

www.egmontusa.com
www.kristihelvig.com

THE LIBRARY OF CONGRESS HAS CATALOGED THE
HARDCOVER EDITION AS FOLLOWS:
Helvig, Kristi.
Burn out / Kristi Helvig.
pages cm
Summary: In the future, when the Earth is no longer easily habitable,
seventeen-year-old Tora Reynolds, a girl in hiding, struggles to protect
weapons developed by her father that could lead to disaster should they
fall into the wrong hands.
ISBN 978-1-60684-479-3 (hardback)
[1. Survival--Fiction. 2. Government, Resistance to--Fiction. 3. Weapons--
Fiction. 4. Mercenary troops--Fiction. 5. Orphans--Fiction. 6. Science fiction.]
I. Title.
PZ7.H37623Bur 2014
[Fic]--dc23
2013018280

Paperback ISBN 978-1-60684-569-1

Printed in the United States of America

For T, C & K
My sun, moon, and stars

• • •

On neither the sun, nor death,
can a man look fixedly.

—FRANÇOIS DE LA ROCHEFOUCAULD

• • •

Chapter ONE

300 years from now

SIX MONTHS AND COUNTING, YET NOT A WHISPER OF A
fellow human to be found. I stared down at the small
device attached to my wrist. The locator light on my Infinity, which would blink if anyone on the planet logged on
to GlobalNet, taunted me with its perpetual darkness.
Though it felt like an exercise in futility, I checked it multiple times a day due to equal parts habit and desperation.
Despite my perseverance, bad thoughts surfaced again. I
had to continually distract myself from my worst fear—
that I was the last girl on Earth.

Weary of the blank screen, I pressed a small button on
the Infinity but hit the wrong one. My little sister's smiling face floated out in front of me. I fought back tears and
quickly punched another button. She disappeared and the

room filled with a moving, three-dimensional image. My happy place. Sunlight reflected off the water's surface and a lime-green fish darted through the waves. Seaweed floated by me as the smell of salt water invaded my nostrils. The sea stretched out in all directions, surrounding me, endless in its reach. I pushed my hand into the bright blue water, desperate to immerse myself in it, yet grasped only air.

The stupid oceans had tricked us all. They weren't endless—they were gone. Most of the people too, after the sun started to burn out a kajillion years ahead of schedule.

The saltwater scent from the program caught my attention again and I focused on the aquamarine water. It was superimposed on the stark walls of the bunker. I lay down and pretended to be submerged in the cool depths as the waves crashed above me. It was somehow harder to catch my breath down here on the imaginary ocean floor. After another minute, the need for oxygen overwhelmed me. I must have done a better job visualizing than I thought. *You're not really on the bottom of the ocean, Tora. Yeah, tell that to my lungs.* I powered off the Infinity and sat upright. The ocean disappeared in an instant. My need to breathe did not.

Breathing was supposed to be the one thing I could count on down here. Maybe there was a leak in the shelter's oxygen line. My lungs burned in protest and my chest ached. I staggered to the front room in search of my helmet, using what little air I had left to curse a blue streak. Most people didn't have to deal with this crap.

Most people were dead.

The steady hum of the generators surrounded me, and provided my only break from the silence. Solar-powered lights flooded the room, making it easy to see the oxygen saturation meter flashing red. The level had dropped twenty percent. Though the oxygen level in the shelter had been erratic for the last twenty-four hours, it hadn't dipped below ninety percent before today.

My father had placed all the important meters in this front room, which was convenient in a twisted way—I could get all the bad news at once. I peered over at the water machine, noting the low level, and more flashing red lights. God, I hated those lights.

I followed the air line across the room to the hole in the ceiling where it exited the shelter. It was intact, which meant the problem lay somewhere aboveground. Perfect— a choice between braving the scorching sun or breathing. Breathing won. My lungs screamed for oxygen. I pulled on the protective sunsuit and twisted my dark hair into a knot before I yanked the helmet down over it. The repair job wouldn't go so well if my hair burst into flames.

Once the helmet snapped in place, the emergency oxygen activated from a small tank inside the suit. When full, the tank could last a few hours tops. I gulped huge mouthfuls of the stale air, then grabbed my father's tool kit and climbed the ladder to the door in the ceiling.

When I pushed open the door and stepped out of the underground shelter onto the surface, dust invaded my throat and my eyes burned from the airborne particles. While my tinted helmet protected me from the harsh light of the sun and provided oxygen, the air filtration system was crap. It was beyond hot out thanks to the sun's ever-expanding size.

Sweat drenched my body within seconds as the intense heat enveloped me. Some early survivors had said this was what hell was like. They were the same ones who claimed the asteroid incident was God's will. Though they preached with righteous indignation about mankind being punished for their wicked ways, they ended up dying just like everyone else. Guess nothing brought out evangelism faster than disaster, but they didn't get that the real hell was Earth.

While trying not to breathe in more dust, I dashed the fifty yards to where the oxygen tubing emerged from the ceiling of the shelter and connected to a converter box in the midst of a monster cactus cluster. My dad took care to keep as much of the line as possible underground, but he couldn't avoid the small part that connected to the plants themselves.

I took care to avoid the massive, knifelike spines of the plants, and inspected the line. A small portion of the outer metal tubing was removed. The inner tube looked as though an animal had chewed through it, thus cutting off the life-saving air to the shelter. I couldn't believe a creature existed that could withstand this environment. Most of the animals had died soon after the plants. Only the giant hyper-evolved cactus had survived—thrived even, and it was the sole oxygen-producing life left in this burned world.

Feeling hotter by the second, I dug through my bag for what I needed. I laughed when I found it, which elicited a coughing fit as I inhaled more of the swirling dust. Of all the advanced technology that allowed my continued survival, what I needed in this case was duct tape. Metallic, heat-resistant duct tape.

I attempted to tear off some tape, but my gloves were too bulky. I checked my wrist gauge—the oxygen tank was ninety-six percent full, and the heat indicator showed I had less than a minute of exposure before bare skin would fry. I stripped off the gloves, then wrapped and double-wrapped the tape around the tubing, before pressing it firmly in place. A searing pain in my right hand startled me, and a large blister popped out on the back of it. I grabbed a coated thermoplastic clamp from the bag, clasped it around the repaired tubing, and ran.

As I sprinted back to the door, two more angry blisters popped up on the back of the same hand. I didn't want to pull the glove back on over my large blister, and now I had three to deal with because of it. Crackling pain shot through my hand. *Please don't let me catch fire.* I yanked at the door but quickly snatched my hand away from the burning hot handle. "Goddammit!"

My father often reminded me to wear gloves when opening the door since the protective, heat-resistant coating on the handle had thinned. Fixing it had been his next project, but getting murdered had caused a major interruption of his to-do list. The door lay flat on the ground, as if only dirt, not a glorified bomb shelter, lay underneath. That was how my father designed it—part of his master survival plan.

I shoved my unburned hand into a glove, jerked the door upward, and scrambled down into the dim light. The door slammed shut behind me and I tripped, tumbling the rest of the way down the ladder. I lay on my back where I fell and stared up at the ceiling. At least I was out of the harsh sunlight. My right hand blazed with pain. When I dared peek at it, a raw, burning mess greeted me. I hoped it would heal quickly. If infection set in, I'd have to dip into my limited supply of antibiotics, because there was no way I'd make it as a lefty.

I filled the sink with only as much warm water as I needed to cover my hand. The meter on my water supply lowered until the red lights turned from flashing to a steady red. Dumb-ass lights. When my tender flesh met the liquid it felt like a thousand burning needles stabbing me at once. A loud sob tore from my throat. I pushed thoughts of Dad from my mind, yet couldn't help thinking that he would have known exactly how to handle this.

I glanced around and spotted the first-aid kit at the end of the counter. If I used the liquid burn treatment and some bandages, maybe I wouldn't need to use the meds. I forced myself to soak my hand for several more minutes. I closed my eyes and tried to imagine that the water was cold, but it was hard to picture something you'd never experienced.

With burn out happening so far ahead of predictions, the heat-resistant technology had barely been in place to create pipes that wouldn't melt into the water. People were too busy dying at the time to care whether the water was cold or not. Sure, I could experience cold by going outside at night when the temperatures were frigid, as long as I didn't mind being ripped apart by the night storms before I froze to death.

The tepid water sloshed over my fingers. I laid my hand gently on a dish towel, careful not to rub off any damaged skin. I dabbed on the burn ointment and gritted my teeth through the pain. After I applied the bandages, I drew a deep breath and peered at the oxygen meter. It had risen to a ninety-four percent saturation level again. Not perfect, but way better than the seventy-four percent it had dropped to thanks to the hole in the line.

It seemed strange that people ever went outside on purpose, even though they had oceans instead of the vast canyons of desert that lay in their place. I'd had enough sunshine today to last me the rest of my life, which likely wouldn't be long anyway. With the dwindling supplies, the chances of making it another six months were slim. I'd be dead before my eighteenth birthday.

As I placed the medical tape and bandages back into the first-aid kit, my eyes fell on the painkiller container. Dad had stocked up on them while he was still able to trade with his contacts in the pod cities. They were the good stuff; the stuff that made you forget about more than your pain. He'd gotten them for my mother, God bless her addicted soul. I remembered a time when my sister and I sat on the couch with her, waiting for the meds to kick in. I sat brushing my sister's hair while she held Mother's hand in her own small one, trying to console her, *Don't worry, Mama. You'll feel good soon.*

For a second, I was tempted. Just one or two tablets under the tongue would ease the scorching pain running through my hand. I slammed the lid shut with my left hand and pushed the kit across the counter. Out of sight, out of mind. I wasn't worried I'd end up an addict like my mother or anything. It's just that the container was full. If I couldn't get off the planet—my Plan A—these meds were my Plan B, and I sure as hell wasn't going to jeopardize Plan B by depleting my overdose supply.

I'd cram the tablets under my tongue as fast as they'd melt, then drink the last bit of water to wash it all down. An easy death. As Plan A seemed less likely with each passing day, I knew I had to prepare myself for Plan B.

I smoothed the bandage across my hand and decided to do the daily bunker check. The routine calmed me, so I walked down the narrow hallway to scan the bedrooms and office before reaching my father's gun room. It's not like things were ever different than the day before, yet seeing the guns secured brought me comfort. After leaving the weapons room, I pressed my hand to the lock and watched with satisfaction as the lock glowed red again.

I returned to the front room and steamed a cup of my mother's favorite herbal tea. Though water had been scarce, she'd insisted that a cup a day held restorative powers for her fragile psyche. As far as I could tell, it was the only thing apart from the meds that brought her any peace. Her smile and joy had dissipated before our eyes soon after we moved to the bunker. The memory of her laughter from when we lived in the pod city faded over time until I wasn't sure I'd ever heard it at all.

The painting on the wall caught my eye, and I straightened it the way I did every day—made it perfect, just like my little sister used to do every time she walked by it. The slight movement caused more pain to shoot through my injured hand. She was so proud of that picture. She'd wanted to make our home prettier and thought it was the best thing she ever painted. It was.

My younger sister would have known squat about burn treatment, but she would have tried to hug my pain away. My chest tightened at memories of her enthusiastic embraces. I squeezed my eyes shut, attempting to blot out their charred bodies. My insides clenched and I gritted my teeth against the feelings welling inside me. I couldn't be weak. *You can't have a pity party; there's no one left to invite.*

I sank down into a chair and glanced down at my Infinity. It was powered by my body's energy, making it a true energetic device, or e-device as the Consulate termed it. I'd laughed at the ad they'd run on the GlobalNet: *Infinity—it doesn't die until you do.* At the time I'd worried they needed better marketing people, but in hindsight, it was the most honest thing that ever came out of their mouths.

Maybe I'd torture myself by checking again for other survivors. My father had rewired my personal locator button so that while I could view the location of others on the Net, no one could see mine. It would only show that someone was online, not where or who I was. This was so the Consulate couldn't find me, or the weapons, but it meant no one else could either. I had this fantasy that there was someone out there who happened to be online every time I wasn't and vice versa. If I stayed on long enough, we'd eventually make contact. Though I still checked often, I hadn't been quite as motivated in the last few weeks. The silence had grown too depressing.

I pushed the button and swore I saw a locator light flash as the device turned on. I blinked and stared hard at the screen. Nothing. My eyes must have been playing tricks on me. I ignored the pain in my hand as I scanned the screen.

A sudden sharp banging on the door overhead made me jump, and my injured hand hit the counter. Blinding pain shot through my arm along with fresh fear. "Dammit!" I grabbed the hand with my good one to still the throbbing.

The pounding on the door sounded rhythmic and human. My mind raced. It wasn't like I could fight someone off with an injured hand, but I had my gun, Trigger, and my father's weapons were secure.

The banging grew insistent. Whoever it was knew someone was home. I squared my shoulders and looked up. At least being killed by a person would be preferable to burning to death on the surface. Maybe that's why they were knocking so loudly—because they were burning alive. With all of my father's brilliance, you'd think he would have thought of putting in a peephole.

Though the external lock was keyed only to my family's vibrations and couldn't be opened by anyone else, there was an extra lock inside—an old-fashioned slide lock. The "just in case" lock, my father had called it. It creaked loudly when opened, but that was part of its purpose.

I crept up a rung on the ladder and yelled at my ceiling. "Who the hell is banging on my door?"

The voice called down to me in a strong but calm tone. It was the voice of someone who was definitely not burning. "Guess who's banging on your door?"

I couldn't help smiling as I whispered my response. "Plan A."

Chapter TWO

"Long time no see, Tora." Markus propped up his brown boots on the thermoplastic-fiber table. He slurped the meager cup of water I'd given him, and his dark hair fell over his eyes.

In spite of my happiness at the sight of another human being, I couldn't help but remind myself that this particular human was Markus. I eyed him with suspicion. "Yeah, I'm surprised you came back."

He was one of a handful of people I'd had contact with since we came to the shelter. Though he was only twenty-one, he had his own ship—almost unheard of outside of the pod cities—and had conducted business with my father on occasion. He'd helped my father transport the weapons to our shelter from the pod city. And despite Markus' illegal business ventures, my father trusted him enough from their dealings that if a new planet was ever found, he wanted Markus to fly us there.

He hadn't trusted Markus on other matters though, and after Markus' hand lingered too long on my back during one visit, he'd warned me about his reputation with women. I guess that with so few females left, he thought he should give them all a try. He'd come by to visit several times after my father's death, but I'd never trusted him much. Markus' main concern was Markus.

He'd taken off on a trip six months ago to check out a nearby solar system, and had stopped by to visit before he left. There'd been rumors that a group of prominent Consulate members had finally found a decent planet. As Markus had never tested his ship for long outside the atmosphere, he wasn't sure it would make it and said he didn't want to be responsible for my death. He told me that if his ship held up and he found the planet, he'd come back. Though Markus could at best be described as shady, I believed his promise that he'd return for me.

In the meantime, I had to figure out what to do with the guns if the planet turned out to be real. There was no way I was bringing them with me and letting them fall into enemy hands. Unfortunately, they were heat-resistant but I could bury them deep in a cactus grove—I just had to make sure I wouldn't need to use them first. I'd waited, and waited, and then waited some more. Even with Markus' crappy old ship, I knew he could have made it to other galaxies and back in a week or two. After several months had passed, I was sure I'd been left to die.

Markus set down the water and pulled out a flask from his jacket. He offered it to me, but I declined. He took a long pull from the silver container before screwing the top back on. "What can I say? It's been a wild ride. I started having mechanical problems with the space drive."

I rolled my eyes. "Whatever." The space-drive technology—something to do with the eleventh dimension, M-theory, and other crap I didn't understand—could bend the space-time continuum. Ships like Markus' could travel between several galaxies in a week, where it used to take several hundred years. The Consulate ships were even faster.

He leaned over across the table and smirked. "Also, it turned out to be harder to find Caelia than you'd think."

I gasped and leaned forward, my heart leaping in my chest. When Markus first told me about the possibility of an Earthlike place, it sounded more myth than fact, like he was just as likely to find a planet inhabited with vampires and unicorns as one with water. "You found Caelia? In the Hydrus system? Is it habitable?"

Markus studied me, enjoying my anticipation. "Yeah, sure as hell is. Water, air, trees, you name it." He gestured at all the contraptions around us that kept me alive in this subterranean tomb.

My mouth hung open at his words. "Seriously?"

He grinned at me. "Yep. And there are colonies everywhere."

"Colonies of people?" The Consulate's first, second, and final exploratory missions had been total busts. They'd given a pathetic speech on GlobalNet, proclaiming that all hope was lost and everyone should prepare for "the end." They even used air quotes when saying "the end" on the broadcast, as if we might confuse it with the end of something more trivial—like water.

Markus laughed. "Of course, people. I wouldn't be this excited if I was talking about cacti."

"How is that possible? They didn't broadcast it on the GlobalNet, so how . . ." The answer hit me like a big red giant. I stared at Markus. "They only told the people inside the pod cities, the rich people." Only the rich were allowed to live in the pod cities. The rest were left to fend for themselves on the outside.

Markus nodded. "They're the only ones who could afford the fee the Consulate charged for passage to Caelia. Plus, I'm guessing their 'planet repopulation plan' hinged on the hope that doctors, scientists, and various other rich, smart people would reproduce. I'm sure they didn't figure any of us would survive long enough to find out about it." He cracked his knuckles. "They figured wrong."

Markus watched my face, which I kept blank. Rage bubbled deep down inside but stayed buried, where emotions should stay. Rage was useless, hope only brought pain, and love ended in death.

He cleared his throat. "I think it's safe to say the human race will continue, although I know you don't think that's necessarily a good thing."

After the oceans dried up and all hell broke loose, the pod cities were designed to provide a safe, comfortable environment for the law-abiding citizens. What a crock. But the rich reacted the same as the poor when a new planet wasn't located. They panicked. Many felt that if the world was ending, there was no need to follow laws. The nickname on the GlobalNet for these people was burners—those who used the sun's burn out as an excuse to be total assholes. Some killed their own family members for an extra cup of water.

I shrugged. "A year alone in this hellhole and suddenly the thought of being with other humans makes me downright giddy." The news broadcast on my Infinity had gone dead shortly after the government reported my father's death. I'd thought the outage meant everyone in the pod cities had died. "Speaking of other humans, I've had no luck trying to find anyone on the GlobalNet. Did you see any signs of any other people?"

Markus crossed his hands behind his head and sighed. "Sweetcakes, I hate to break it to you, but I'm pretty sure it's just the two of us down here. It's nothing but wasteland as far as I can see from my ship. Even our pod city looked deserted."

I blinked away tears. Sector 5, where we lived, used to be the continental United States before the oceans dried up and Earth became one giant, happy continent. Now there were only sectors. Each of the six sectors had a pod city, with the Consulate members scattered among the cities to help "maintain order." If the other sectors were as empty as ours, we really could be the last two people on Earth.

He looked at me and leaned forward. "It's been difficult for you, hasn't it?"

Unbelievable. Did he really think I was going to spill my guts to him? My eyes fell on my sister's painting on the wall behind him. Wildflowers. Colorful flowers that didn't exist in our world. She'd been so determined to make them come to life again somehow. Though we'd had a few decorations in our place in the pod city, she couldn't have remembered that house—I barely remembered it myself.

My sister had begged me to look up pictures of flowers on my Infinity. She'd been obsessed with them and thought they were the loveliest of all extinct things. It bothered her that we didn't have real ones. The cactus flowers were the closest thing, but their white petals sat high atop the limbs and my sister complained she couldn't see them from the ground. I used to worry she'd try to climb up the cactus and impale herself on one of the giant spines.

The fact that the only thing providing oxygen could also kill us pretty much summed up our world. She'd made the painting the week before she died.

So yeah, things had been hard, but I wasn't telling Markus that. The fact that he might be the only man left on Earth didn't make him any less slimy. But since he was my ticket out of here, I produced a wistful smile. "Yeah, it's hard without them. I miss my sister . . . and despite everything, my father was a great man." *Unlike you.*

His attempt at a caring smile was pathetic. I cut him off before he could say anything else. "What about you, Markus? Still running guns—or have you run out of people to run them to?" He'd sold illegal weapons ever since he figured out how to fly his dead father's ship. And thanks to the Consulate laws, all weapons were illegal, so he had plenty of business. His father had been in the same line of work, and though Markus never spoke of his untimely death, I figured it had something to do with his job description.

This made him laugh. "You're right that my prospects are . . . drying up . . . here on Earth." He paused, delighted in his joke. "But Caelia is a new place and the colonies are trying to establish themselves. They're mighty unstable right now. Lucky for me, man may travel far and wide, but he still loves his guns."

"So, you mean it's Earth all over again." I sighed. "The more things change, the more they stay the same."

He laughed. "You watch too many old GlobalNet shows—sometimes you talk like you're hundreds of years old. Yes, it's like Earth, minus the astronomical temperatures. Caelia's sun is where ours was back before the 'roid hit it." Markus smashed his fist into his palm like I needed a visual. He smirked. "People are already soaking up the rays—right next to the oceans."

While I had no intention of lying out in the sun on any planet, the thought of standing knee-deep in an ocean of water transfixed me. Almost every day, I gazed with longing at the three-hundred-year-old picture on my Infinity, taken before things escalated and destroyed any chance that future generations would see water. I yearned for water. So much so that I would do almost anything to get Markus to take me there. There was only one thing I wouldn't do. I had promised my father that in the weeks before his death.

Of course it was the one thing Markus wanted. "Come on, Tora. You know why I'm here. What are you going to do with all those guns? Be reasonable."

Why couldn't he have asked me for sex? Although dying was only slightly less preferable to having sex with Markus, I could've at least strung him along until I figured out an alternative. Disgusting, I could handle. Betraying my father, I couldn't.

I realized I could hand over the guns to Markus and be zipping along to Caelia within a few hours. But at what cost? Bringing weapons of mass destruction to a new world wasn't what I wanted for my family's legacy. I'd rather die than see the guns fall into his hands.

I shook my head. "You know I can't do that. My father—"

"Your father made these guns for the Consulate," he pointed out.

He was right. As conditions spiraled over the last three hundred years, scientists frantically tried to develop ways to reverse the sun situation—most recently, my dad. It wasn't until Dad told the Consulate that there was no hope that they changed his assignment to weapons creation. They told him it was in case they ran across hostile foreign species while they searched for greener pastures. Liars.

"Yeah, before he realized what they were going to be used for. Then he regretted it so much, he spent the rest of his life making sure people like you didn't get your hands on them." I clenched my fists, ignoring the pain that pulsed through them. "That's why he made sure they wouldn't work for anyone but me."

Markus looked surprised by my last statement. Apparently Dad hadn't told him about how he rekeyed all the triggers. Oops. Guess I shouldn't have mentioned that part. His eyes narrowed. After a long, hard look at me, he took his feet off the table and pushed back his seat.

I gulped and thought fast. "The Consulate left you on the outside to die just like the rest of us. Still, I'm guessing that's who you want to sell the guns to. Why deal with those creeps?"

"Survival. To use one of your old quotes, 'If you can't beat 'em, join 'em.' Don't you want off this planet? I'll take you to Caelia right now. You won't die here, all alone. All I'm asking for in return is the guns. Do you have any idea how much money we could make if we sold them?" He stood and took a step toward me.

He was a good head taller and had at least eighty pounds on me. I knew what he was thinking. My heart skidded in my chest, and sweat broke out on my brow. Act tough. I couldn't show fear or he'd win. Luckily, my father had taught me well. I leaned forward on the table and crossed my legs so that my right leg reached over my left. Trigger was tucked into my right boot but I didn't want to risk dropping it with my bandaged right hand.

I smiled up at Markus. "I think I will have a swig of that paint thinner after all."

"That's my girl." He looked down to grab the flask. "It's quite tasty if I do say so—"

Taking advantage of the distraction, I used my left hand to pull the gun out of my boot and pointed it at his head. "Okay, asshole. You can leave now."

Markus put his hands up in surrender, but didn't look very scared. The fact that he didn't even bring a gun meant he didn't expect a fight. In fact, he smiled. "Have you ever actually shot anyone? I'm guessing not."

The irony wasn't lost on me that I was using a gun to protect other guns from burners who would use them against me. Still, I was the one aiming a gun at some-one. *Say something else before he realizes how scared you are.* "You wanna find out? I can shoot well enough with my left hand—and I've got endless ammo in case I miss the first time." I hoped he didn't notice the faint tremble in my hand.

Markus kept his hands above him. "Do you really need a gun to solve this?"

I flashed a coy smile and batted my eyes, trying to ignore the tightness in my throat. "My father told me a girl should never be alone with a boy without protection." I held Trigger steady. "What can I say? I'm a careful girl." I gestured toward the door with a flick of my head. "Now get out."

He took a step backward but didn't seem ready to give up. "How exactly do you think you're going to get off this planet without me, Tora? I promised your dad that if anything happened to him, I'd look out for you. Don't be crazy."

I snorted. "Crazy? I was crazy to think you came back here to help me. Did you promise my dad you'd steal his guns too? No, you only came back because you either thought I was already dead, leaving all of these guns for the taking, or you were hoping I'd be so desperate to leave here that I'd do anything."

I stood and took a step toward him, not lowering Trigger. Anger replaced my fear. "So maybe I was crazy to think you had a decent bone in your body. I can see I was wrong —you're a total burner. I don't know why my dad didn't see it. I should kill you right now." I hoped he wouldn't call my bluff, because I hadn't killed a thing in my life. Even though he deserved it, I wasn't sure I could take him out.

Markus frowned, but took another step backward and bumped into the ladder leading up to the door. "I'm a man of opportunity, always have been. Your dad tended to see the best in people and might have overestimated my character. Still, I think offering to take you with me was pretty decent of me. I won't be back again, you know. This is your last chance."

I wanted to kick myself for wasting a glass of water on

him. I pressed Trigger's engagement button. It instantly recognized my energy and glowed a soft blue color. "I don't want to hear another word from you or I'll start shooting, I swear it."

Markus turned, helmet in hand, and scampered up the ladder. He pushed on the door and glaring reddish light flooded the chamber. I held my bandaged hand to my eyes to shield them from the sun, but kept Trigger aimed at his retreating form. He turned back to look at me for a second. I couldn't tell if it was scorn or pity I saw in his eyes before he pulled his helmet down. The door slammed shut, blocking the sun.

I kept the gun pointed at the ceiling until my hand grew sore. After some time passed, I powered it down and placed it on the kitchen table. I sank into my chair and rested my head on the table.

Markus was gone and he was never coming back. That burner was my last hope for getting off of this rock.

Damn.

Chapter THREE

THE WINDS WAILED THROUGHOUT THE NIGHT. THE HOWLING penetrated every nook of the shelter and echoed inside my sleep chamber. Though it was impossible, I could have sworn my sleep pad, which hung from the ceiling, swayed underneath me from the breeze. I shuddered as I lay awake in the dark, yet there was an odd comfort in the sound. Something about the noise made me feel I wasn't alone.

Three weeks had passed since Markus left, and I had no doubt that he'd told the truth for once and had no intention of stepping foot on Earth again. He was probably passed out somewhere on Caelia after a night of boozing.

Maybe I could have risked letting Markus take the guns with him, and then tried to dump them in space, but something told me he would have found a way to overpower me. No way could I let those guns move to a new world. On the plus side, I didn't have to consider having sex with him, and my father's guns were safe. Even though they wouldn't work for anyone else, I didn't want to take any chances that someone could reprogram them the way Dad did. I'd find a way to get rid of them before I offed myself. I was back to Plan B.

The shrieking in the air continued. The nights had grown increasingly violent in temperament, as though they could fight off the sun's endless assault on the dark. The sun was much bigger than it had been when there were oceans, its brilliant shade of red quite unlike the small, golden-yellow sun I'd read about on the GlobalNet. After it finished its vast expansion, it would devour Earth before shrinking to nothing. Not that there'd be anything alive here to witness it.

After tossing and turning for hours, I finally drifted into sleep.

My sister's voice permeated my dreams, and a small hand tugged at my shirt. "Come on, Tora. I wanna play hide-and-seek." I blinked and sat up, confused, struggling to make out her features in the dark room. Her eyes gave off a strange glow, but before I could get a better look, she giggled and ran away from me. "I'm going to hide. Count to ten," she called. I got to my feet, but frowned. We weren't in the shelter anymore. We were back in our pod in the city, but something seemed off. It was daytime—the room should be lighter.

Laughter echoed through the pod and her singsong voice sounded like it was coming from everywhere. "You'll never find me." I heard the click of the front door.

"No," I yelled. "You shouldn't go outside." I shook off my fog and ran down the hall, but stopped short in the front room. There was no furniture, no anything. The room was completely bare. My pulse quickened and I hurried out the door, shouting her name.

Stark white pods lined the grids in neat rows. Bright light flooded the city through the dome. Though it consisted of a special substance that muted the sun's damaging rays, the Consulate still discouraged people from going outside for long. They didn't understand that my sister craved the outdoors the way my mother craved pain meds. A slight breeze stirred due to the main wind generator that continuously pumped recycled air through the dome.

I looked behind our father's land cruiser, one of her usual spots. She wasn't there. I called her name but was met with silence. Her girlish laughter had disappeared. My sister didn't do quiet, and I began to panic. I turned around, looking in all directions to no avail. No one was there. Though it couldn't yet be night, the sky suddenly dimmed, and the pod dwellings cast long shadows on the streets. I broke into a cold sweat, my heart hammering. The air went still, and the light faded to dark gray. I screamed her name into the night, my voice hoarse. Then everything plunged into blackness. I was alone.

My eyes flew open. I was back in the shelter, my body

curled into a fetal position and my face damp with tears. Don't think about her. A large, dry lump had lodged itself in my throat. I flicked tears from my face; it wasn't like they could bring her back. Plus, crying was a luxury I couldn't afford given the state of my water supply.

I finally managed to swallow. The familiar burning sensation returned to my throat. Chronic thirst, my trusty companion.

The water situation hadn't become life-threatening until the last few decades. Everyone became obsessed with water, as death by dehydration was not a pretty way to go. When the ponds, lakes, and finally, the oceans had boiled and evaporated, the Consulate scientists came through with technology allowing us to glean the precious water molecules from the atmosphere. You had to give them credit for that I guess.

The technology was termed Water in Air Recycling, W.A.R., and the acronym said it all. People fought and killed one another over these machines—not everyone could afford them but you needed one to survive for long. My father said it was all-out civil war in the early years. It didn't stop until all of the have-nots literally died of thirst.

I padded across the small room and checked the W.A.R.: same level as yesterday. The water output had continued its gradual decline, yet I was still able to enjoy a whopping two and a half cups of water per day. My father's murder had seen to that.

The machines worked great around the time when

everything had just evaporated—there were tons of water molecules in the air. As the years went on, the sun grew hotter and the molecules scarcer. Despite the shortage, my father improved the detection levels on our W.A.R., and though we were never in danger of it overflowing, we always had enough to drink. It wasn't until I was about ten years old that we noticed the difference. We'd check the level in the morning and there would be an inch less water produced than the week before. We were forced to ration our drinking water until we were each down to one cup of water a day. It was terrible that on the day my mother and sister died, one of the first thoughts to cross my mind after the mind-numbing grief was "more water for me."

Next up on my checklist was the oxygen rating: ninety-three percent saturation level. I exhaled slowly. Hopefully, it had reached a stable level after my repair job. If it continued going down, it would be a problem. I knew it would eventually decline over time, along with the H_2O molecules in the atmosphere, but I wasn't sure how low it could get before I'd have problems breathing. Whenever it did happen, I'd take care of myself long before my lungs gave out.

I grabbed a gel-filled energy packet, one of my two "meals" of the day, and considered what to do. The options were underwhelming. For months, I'd constantly been on the GlobalNet trying to find other survivors and was grateful for my father's Infinity. The Consulate had given it to him as a gift for creating the weapons; however, instead of a thank-you note, my father took his guns and fled.

I still checked each day for signs of life on my Global-Net page, Surviving Burn Out. I used to write a daily entry but had since been recycling my original post:

Hello, fellow burn out survivors. Congratulations on still being here. I thought I'd share what I know about how we got to this desolate state. If you already know all this, or if science hurts your brain, just skip to the comments and talk to me. Please.

It started three hundred years ago when a world-ending rock hurtled toward Earth. In a last-ditch effort to save our planet from the largest asteroid ever recorded, the then-government tried a crazy idea. The idea worked. Sort of. They successfully hit the asteroid with a rocket and diverted it.

Dad said the problem was where it ended up. The huge, moon-sized mass was accidentally sent straight into the sun, which would have been fine, except this particular asteroid contained more dark matter than scientists had seen before. An unexpected reaction occurred and the sun kicked into hyperdrive. It began burning hydrogen like crazy, and before anyone could comprehend what had happened, the helium in the core was exhausted. It went downhill from there. Anyway, Dad was the final scientist tapped by the Consulate to see if there was any possibility of reversing the burn out. Turns out there wasn't. Even supersmart scientist guys

*can't outsmart Mother Nature. If you're reading this, feel
free to share your survival tips. Or, you know, just say
hi. Anyone else out there tired of sunsuits?*

Keep on living—Tora

I had no subscribers and had yet to see a comment. If
everyone weren't dead, I'd take it personally.

I stared at the Infinity. It reminded me of the first and
last time I encountered an actual Consulate member. We'd
been living in the pod city and I'd begged Dad to take me
with him to work one day. I must have been nine or so at
the time, and needed a break from the monotony of the pod.
Visitors weren't usually allowed into his office building, but
Dad gave in to my whining. We climbed in his cruiser and
took off through the pod city toward the Consulate head-
quarters. All I could see aside from other cruisers were the
rows of pods. Even though we lived in a city, I rarely saw
other people unless they were going from their cruiser into
their pod homes and vice versa. My sister was the only ren-
egade who ran outside whenever she could.

I'd never been to the center of the city and stared wide-
eyed at a large electronic billboard that flashed Consulate
messages like "Pumping Air Because We Care." We neared
the main Consulate building and slowed at the gated entry,
where a three-dimensional virtual keyboard popped out of
thin air. Dad punched in a code and the gate swung open.
We parked the cruiser and walked to the building entrance
where another keyboard appeared.

I frowned. "Why do they need so much security?"

Dad punched in more numbers and pulled me inside. "It's not safe to talk about it right now. Just don't draw attention to yourself."

I stared at him quizzically but kept silent. What wasn't safe? I mean we were inside the Consulate building so I couldn't imagine a safer place in the whole city. The Consulate protected us and provided air. Maybe they were worried about people breaking in to the building and stealing things—it would certainly explain their discouragement of visitors.

The halls and floor shone as if everything had just been polished. I stepped carefully, afraid I might slip, but my shoes held their grip on the glossy surface. We passed several others in the hallway who wore badges similar to my father's. A few nodded at him, and passed cursory glances in my direction.

"There sure isn't a lot of chitchat here, is there?" I observed.

"Shhhh. We're almost there." He guided me around a corner.

The feminine voice seemed to come from everywhere. "Please keep your badges visible at all times. Help the Consulate help you to stay safe." It took me a second to realize it was an automatic recording projected through a sound system.

We stopped at a small door and Dad waved his hand over a lock. The door slid open and we stepped inside a small, perfectly square room. It was as blindingly white as the hallway. The door closed soundlessly behind us.

I stared at the stark walls. "They're not big on color here, huh?"

Dad sighed. "They don't want people distracted from their work. Color and artwork is a violation of code 203b."

"Geez. That seems like a dumb rule."

Dad put a finger to his lips but smiled as he pointed at a small device in the ceiling. "All the offices are monitored to ensure adequate compliance with assigned work duties."

I stared at the small object above us. "So they can see me anyway. They know I'm here."

"Yes, having outsiders in the facility is a violation of code 417c. I'm sure I'll get a documented warning about this." He didn't sound very upset.

I hadn't realized the codes were so strict or that he had risked a job warning. "Dad, I didn't mean for you to get in trouble."

Dad pulled up a three-dimensional keyboard and logged in. "No, it's time for you to see this . . . see how things are." He waved a hand in my direction. "I need to get a few things done and then I want to show you something."

I paced around the bare room for a while as he typed away. A strange pent-up energy overcame me and I hopped up and down several times.

Dad looked over with a frown. "What are you doing?"

I kept running. "I feel weird . . . like overly energetic or something."

Dad's eyebrows raised. "Oh, that. Must be the extra oxygen they pump in here."

I stopped running. Oxygen was a rare commodity. I stared at Dad.

"They think additional oxygen keeps employees more energized and alert during the workday. Based on your spontaneous workout, I'd say they're onto something."

His eyes stopped me before I asked the obvious: *Where did they get extra air?*

The voice appeared out of nowhere again. "Mr. Reynolds, please report to Mr. Davis, and bring your guest with you."

Crap. They'd definitely noticed me. It couldn't be good that they wanted to see us.

Dad stood and motioned for me to join him. I realized I was sweating and not just from my run.

I gripped his arm. "Are we in trouble?" I whispered.

"Don't worry. We're fine." He waved his hand over the lock and the office door slid open.

Why did he sound so sure of himself? Didn't he realize that they could fire him? Without a job, we couldn't afford to stay in the pod city. We could be kicked out like the others, which would mean certain death.

I stuck by his side as we moved down several more hallways before we came to the end of a hall with an oversized door. The door slid open without any help from us.

"Come in, Micah, come in." A large man sat behind an equally large desk and waved my father in. A thin woman with frosted hair and dark lipstick sat in a chair to his side. She had the air of an entitled assistant. She gave me a tight-lipped smile and folded her hands in her lap. They both wore bright orange badges with *Consulate* stamped on them in dark black lettering. It contrasted with Dad's small white employee badge.

Dad sat in one of two empty chairs in front of them, so I parked myself in the other one.

The man's booming voice rang out again. "And who do we have here?" His eyes appraised me and something about his look made my stomach cringe.

My dad laughed. "Allan, you really don't see the resemblance? This is my oldest daughter, Tora. She is very interested in the work I do and wanted to see it firsthand."

"Yes, sir," I chimed in. "It's my dream to work for the Consulate one day." The lie came easily.

"Well, we don't normally allow visitors but I'm always happy to hear that someone wants to serve our great cause. It's nice to meet you, Tora." Allan extended his hand in my direction.

I hesitated but leaned over and shook it. His moist, meaty skin clung to mine and I fought the urge to rip myself away. He gave me a good strong squeeze, then released me. When he turned his focus on Dad, I wiped my hand on my pants.

"So, Micah. I was quite impressed with the weapons demonstration you did for us yesterday. I assume the time-line is still on schedule."

My father smiled. "Absolutely. In fact, the timeline is better than expected. I haven't been down to the weapons lab today, but will double-check some of the gun capabilities tomorrow."

"Excellent. So everything will be ready by the end of the summer?"

"Yes, sir."

I glanced over at the assistant and the same smile was pasted across her face. She looked almost frozen until her mouth moved.

"Do you think it might move along even faster if we brought in some help for you?" She managed to speak and smile at the same time.

Dad's jaw clenched but he recovered quickly. "No. As you know, the work I do is highly sensitive. I couldn't promise the same level of confidentiality if others were involved. I'd hate to think what would happen if this sort of information leaked out. . . ."

"No, no, that would have terrible implications," Allan said and threw a piercing gaze at the woman. "Our original deadline is fine. Let us know if there's anything you need."

It was the first time I realized that Dad's weaponry work was of the top secret variety. He'd mentioned making peacekeeping weapons, and it had crossed my mind that weapons and peace didn't seem to go together but who was I to question him? I also realized how valuable Dad was to the Consulate. No wonder he didn't seem concerned about being fired.

Allan opened a drawer in his desk. "Micah, I want you to know how much we appreciate your years of tremendous service to us. We've taken the liberty to add additional funds to your currency chip. I hope you will find it to your satisfaction. We would also like to give you this as a small token of appreciation." He held out a device to my father.

"Thank you, Allan. I'm proud to serve the Consulate in any way I can."

We stood and I moved toward the door before Allan could touch my hand again. I turned once before leaving and the woman's smile remained. I shuddered.

On the ride home, I asked Dad what he'd wanted to show me.

"The weapons room . . . but I decided today wasn't the right time." He sighed. "Soon though." He reached into his bag and tossed me the gift he'd received from Allan. "It's an Infinity."

"Whoa." I stroked the small device and immediately attached it to my wrist. I'd heard of them but had never seen one. Most people had basic GlobalNet tablets, but only a lucky few had the Infinity. I'd even read that people could access books and videos from hundreds of years ago on these things.

I punched a button and a glowing, virtual keyboard appeared in front of me. "This is awesome."

Dad flashed a weary smile. "It's yours."

I gasped. "No way. Thanks, Dad."

"Sure, I need to make a few modifications on it first, but

I think you'll find it useful. Especially once we relocate."

I was so mesmerized by the graphics of the pictures in front of me that it took a minute for his words to sink in. I turned my head. "Relocate?"

"Yeah," Dad said. "We're moving."

That same week, Dad had started moving the guns out and used his "bonus money" to build our bunker. I'd overheard late-night whispers between him and Mom about something "bad." All I knew was that whatever he was doing, the Consulate didn't know about it. He told my sister and me that we couldn't tell a soul about our moving, and three short months later, we arrived at our new home sweet home. My weapons training with him had started almost immediately.

• • •

I ran my hand over the Infinity and smiled wistfully. Guess it couldn't hurt to check for survivors again. A light flashed off as I turned on the machine. The locator light. No way could I have imagined it twice. Someone had to be out there.

After an hour staring at the screen, my eyes got blurry. Hope took a nosedive when it occurred to me that both times I'd seen the light flash had been when I'd turned on the device. The light itself was probably defective. Fabulous.

I considered watching one of my favorite old shows but pulled up my sister's favorite program instead. A three-dimensional field of wildflowers instantly surrounded me.

I lay down on the floor amidst the carpet of blossoms. She and I would lie for hours as the flowers waved around us in the gentle wind, a breeze so unlike the harsh winds we experienced in our world. We'd watch butterflies land on the colorful petals before taking flight again, inhale the lush fragrances, and pretend this wild garden was our front yard. The scent of the flowers was the best part of the program—it almost made it real. Instead of rocks and dust, we had fields of flowers and the ocean as our landscapes. This was how we spent our time, rather than worrying about school.

Though there hadn't been formal schooling in decades due to lack of enrollment, the pod cities provided online tutorials in basic subjects. My sister and I stopped all the lessons except Spanish once we moved out of the pod city. It seemed ridiculous to learn about history when we had no future.

We kept up with the Spanish though because the Consulate frowned upon all languages except English. It made us feel like rebels to turn on the Infinity program and discuss the *bellas flores*. For hours at a time, we lost ourselves in fantasy worlds involving flowers and oceans.

I turned my head to track an *abeja* skittering from flower to flower. It flew closer toward me, so close that I flinched despite knowing it couldn't sting me.

I sat and turned off the device. The flowers disappeared into thin air.

PING! PING!

The strange sound jarred me. I cocked my head to listen, my ear tilted up toward the ceiling. The wind had died down, so it couldn't be something blowing against the shelter.

PING! PING!

The noise sounded like it was coming from directly above me. Maybe it was the same animal that had chewed through my oxygen line, though I still didn't understand how it could survive out here. If so, I had to get up there and take care of it before it did more damage. But what if Markus had come back? What if the lure of such high-tech weaponry was too tempting to resist? Either way, I'd have to strap on my entire protective suit. Another burn would not be pretty. I wriggled into my suit, and winced as the glove slid over my hand. Ready, I grabbed Trigger and powered her up.

I climbed the ladder, then hesitated at the top rung underneath the door.

PING! PING!

Something was definitely hitting the door. My heart raced. This could go very badly, but I didn't make it to seventeen by being an apocawuss. I braced myself, took a deep breath, and pushed the door open. I jumped out and kept the gun in front of me while scanning the area. Nothing looked unusual. In fact, there was nothing but dirt, boulders, and cacti as far as the eye could see. A large boulder sat ten feet to my left, and another group of huge rocks stood at least fifty feet away.

The cacti to my right, descendants of the saguaros, were fifty feet tall and six feet across. Their crazy-sharp spines looked like they could do some serious damage. The roots grew forty feet underground. These plants provided some major oxygen, which is why my dad built the shelter near a cluster of them. The oxygen line I'd repaired looked fine, the reflective duct tape gleaming in the sunlight. There was nothing hostile to be found, save for the sun, and it was always hostile.

I watched and waited, but I didn't hear anything. Strange. After another minute, I relaxed. How stupid do you look pointing a gun at a rock? Sweat ran in rivulets down my protective suit, as I roasted in the dark reddish light.

Screw this. I leaned down to pull up the door and go inside. That's when I noticed them.

Several pebbles were scattered around the shelter door. Almost as if they'd been thrown by someone—

"Now!" a voice yelled.

I dove behind the boulder to my left, barely escaping the several rounds of lasers that sprayed the rock.

After a moment, the rapid fire ceased, and I peeked around the side of the stone. Not two, three, or even four, but five sunsuited figures emerged from behind the rocks in the distance. Five bright-white suits headed for my faded red one. They had their guns aimed right at my boulder. I gripped Trigger tight and swallowed hard.

I recognized the swagger of one of the suits, even though he was still some distance away.

Oh, how sweet.

Markus brought friends.

Chapter FOUR

Apparently Markus thought I wouldn't shoot at an old friend, even if said friend shot at me first. He was so wrong. I touched the small trigger panel and shot a stream of electric blue pulses his way. He and one of the other suits flattened themselves to the ground, crawling back toward the rock they came from. How fitting. The other three dashed back behind the second one. A chill ran through me as I realized my rock was the rock—the one where my father found my sister and mother dead. Where they'd been turned into human cinders.

"Tora, it's me, Markus. Don't shoot!" his voice shouted through my helmet com.

Was he kidding? "Oh, sorry, Markus. Was that supposed to be friendly fire? I must have gotten confused, with those lasers coming at me and all."

He stood up, still holding the gun, but in a relaxed pose with his hand off the trigger. "Come on. You know what I'm here for—I'm not leaving without the guns."

I called back. "You know they won't work for you. Trust me; they'll never work for you."

"What do I care? I'm not the one that'll be using them, but I'm getting an unbelievable payment from the ones who will be."

"Payment big enough to erase the guilt of killing an innocent girl?" I asked, my finger on the trigger panel. The gun hummed softly in my hand.

Markus laughed and called back, "Innocent girls don't curse the way you do. And I'm not trying to kill you, just disable you a bit; the Consulate needs you alive. But yes, they're giving me an Unlimited Currency Chip for the guns."

I wanted to kick myself for telling him about being the sole person who could fire them. Markus would likely kill children, if any were left, for a UCC. With so few people remaining after the massive die-offs, a move was made to change to a united global government, coined the Consulate, an international currency system, and an international language. Good thing I already spoke English or I would have been *muy* screwed.

Markus and I faced each other, about fifty yards of dirt between our rock fortresses. This would have been cute if we'd been six years old.

"So, my father's guns for a UCC. Our esteemed Consulate has already declared itself the ruler of Caelia?" I guessed that not only was Markus' desire for the weapons at the behest of the government, they'd probably financed this whole attack. They really wanted the guns.

"Something like that," Markus said.

Everyone had currency chips implanted in their arms that denoted their net worth. If you were poor, you still got the implant but received a minuscule currency amount—the equivalent of space-age welfare. Currency Chips (CC's) were how people obtained the W.A.R.'s when the water ran out. No currency left on your CC, no water.

I got lucky because my dad was the guy who created bioenergetic warfare. Dad didn't have a UCC, but he was rich. He cashed in the bulk of his CC balance on all the equipment he could get from his friends in the pod cities. Luckily, he spent most of it before the Consulate realized he wasn't giving over the guns and zeroed out his chip. I'd say they won in the end though, because Dad was dead.

"Wow, Markus, there must be so much use for it on Caelia. What are you gonna buy . . . an ocean? The whole planet?"

This elicited a laugh from him. "I like that idea. The whole planet. We'll have to see about that."

Movement caught my eye and I ducked down as another spray of blasts hit the rock.

"Crap, I missed her." A female voice. She sounded about my age, which surprised me. A man shooting at me didn't surprise me. Maybe that wasn't fair to all men, but many of the male survivors had been brutes. But a girl burner? Another shot came from that direction, and I pressed the trigger panel on my gun. Blue sparks lit up the rock around them. A small chunk of the rock blasted into the air from the laser and fell to the ground nearby.

I sent the streaming blue light toward Markus before he could shoot again. He dove just in time and I sank back behind the rock. With five of them and only one of me, the odds were not in my favor. My only advantage was a kick-ass gun, but five regular guns seemed like a lot at the moment. I wished I had my favorite super-gun right now, but that bad boy was in storage.

My lungs labored for air despite the oxygen in my suit. Sweat poured down my body and dripped into my eyes, yet I couldn't remove my helmet to wipe my face. The sun was cooking me from the inside out. I was *muy caliente*, and not in the good way. Damn, I was thirsty. All I wanted was to get back underground, bolt the door, and get some water, but the door was a good ten feet away. I'd have to turn my back to the group to open the door and they'd put laser holes in me faster than you could say *agua*.

I yelled from behind my rock. "Where's your ship, dirt-bag?"

"I didn't bring mine . . . it barely made the trip last time. The one I hitched a ride in is over the ridge," he called back. "You wanna give up yet, sweetcakes? You're a little outnumbered in case you didn't notice."

"Fat chance. I'm guessing you burners will be the ones giving up." The ridge was over a half mile behind them. That meant they must be even hotter and thirstier than I was. Maybe they'd be forced to leave soon if I could keep them at a standstill. What I wouldn't give to get to that ship, but it wouldn't do me much good. I couldn't fly it myself. I'd need the dirtbag to pilot it, and I didn't see any way that was going to happen.

I heard the sound before it registered. A roar that grew louder each second. The air kicked up around me and the red light of the sun blazed with anger. Terrific. A sun storm. I stashed the gun in my pants, dug my fingers underneath the rock, and hung on for dear life. The fierce solar winds ripped through, whipping one of the larger pebbles by my door into the side of my suit. It made sharp contact with one of my ribs, and I yelped in pain. I really hoped it wasn't fractured—another medical issue was the last thing I needed.

My suit wove itself back together again where the rock had pierced it. At least the high-tech material would protect me from oxygen loss. I could easily die from their lasers, but I'd be breathing up until the bitter end.

The shrieking of the winds intensified and my body lifted as the gusts threatened to take me for a one-way ride. I gripped the underside of the rock tighter, fighting to hang on, my hands so sweaty I was afraid they'd slip right out of the gloves. Small rocks continued their assault, plunking the sides of my helmet. It didn't help that I couldn't stop coughing from the crap flying through my lousy filtration system. The muscles in my arm burned. I didn't know how much longer I could hold on.

A strong surge yanked me off the ground and I held on with every ounce of strength I had left. I yelled in frustration, and soon realized I wasn't the only one yelling. A body flew past me. Someone had lost their battle with the storm. I craned my neck and watched as the body was flung higher and higher into the air, like a rag doll. It must have been fifty feet in the air when it got caught in the wind shear. The wind slammed it straight into the cactus grove. Several of the sharp spines drove clear through the body, pinning it halfway up the cactus. It didn't move, and I guessed it wasn't going to.

Still clinging to the rock, my only thought was a selfish one.

The odds just got a little better.

Chapter FIVE

THE SUN STORM SEEMED TO LAST FOR AN ETERNITY. FROM the safe confines of the shelter, these storms didn't seem quite as deadly. Things were sure different when you were smack ass in the middle of it. The screaming of the wind gradually subsided to mild whimpers, with occasional defiant gusts mixed in, as though daring me to come out. I relaxed my hold on the rock and touched my side where I'd been hit. Tender and sore, but not broken. I groaned at the deep ache beneath my ribs.

"That you whimpering, Tora? You know they already have a hospital on Caelia."

I yelled back at him. "You won't need a hospital by the time I'm finished with you, Markus!"

A deeper male voice called out. The voice belonged to

boulder number two, which was where the body had flown from. "Miss, um, Reynolds is it? We suffered an injury during the storm and would like permission to check on our man's status. Can we have a cease-fire?"

I looked at the motionless body in the air, hanging from the spikes. "Our man's" status. Then it wasn't the girl that died. "Mr., um, Assassin, is it? There's nothing to check. You didn't suffer an injury; you suffered a fatality. If you insist, be my guest, but I will shoot you in the back." I clutched my weapon, bracing for more gunfire.

"For Attila's sake!" His sigh was audible, despite the distance between us. What kind of name was Attila? Markus must not have warned him about me. Maybe the man had been expecting a frightened, desperate mouse of a girl. I was not that girl.

"Come on, Tora." No way. The girl was trying to reason with me. "Look, we want the guns and we're not leaving without them. There's no reason for anyone else to die."

You mean anyone except me. The odds were still four to one—four too many for my liking.

I yelled back, "Little girl, you sure have been out here an awfully long time in the hot sun . . . thirsty yet?" I knew I'd hit a nerve when she fell silent. They were thirsty. I only had to outlast them. I licked a drip of sweat that fell from my nose onto my lip. If I made it back underground, I was going to drink my entire day's ration in one sitting.

"Give us a break. We'll all die if we sit out here much longer."

"You first, Markus."

The sun started to sink in the sky. Within a few hours, the small sliver of night would emerge. Instead of dying of heat, we'd die quickly from the rapid descent into arctic temperatures—if the night storms didn't get us first. Maybe I could make a break for the door and hole up for the night. If they made it back to the ship in time, we could start the fun all over again in the morning.

More roaring sounded overhead and dust swirled at my feet. This was not possible. Sun storms never happened this close together, and it was too early for the night storms. The noise thundered louder in my ears and the wind picked up speed. Light blazed in my eyes and I shielded them from the glare. When I looked again, I found that this particular blinding light wasn't coming from the sun.

It came from the sun reflecting off the metal of a ship.

A gigantic ship.

The monstrosity veered closer, before hovering over the ridge where Markus and company had parked their craft. The jerks had called for reinforcements. The hand that held my gun shook. This was it. Game over. The odds had been stacked against me anyway, but this ship knocked the whole stack on its ass. I was going to die here, in the same spot as my mother and sister. But I wasn't going to die without a fight. I raised my gun, and peered out from behind the rock.

The ship's engine revved as it came full throttle toward us.

Markus yelled, "What the—?" He stood upright, ripe for the shooting. I placed my finger on the firing switch of the gun and took a breath. I aimed at Markus who faced away from me, staring at the ship.

The ship fired. Pulses of orange light rained down on the ground ahead of me, apparently targeting Markus and his friends. The pulses of light came closer. Yeah, they were definitely aiming for the white suits, which made me glad to be in a red one. Markus hesitated a second before running full speed toward me. Another white suit followed close behind. The two behind the other boulder stood, glanced at Markus, and also raced in my direction. What the hell? Did they think I could protect them from the monstrous ship in the air? They were the military-looking types, not me. That's when it hit me. They weren't running toward me. They were running toward the door. My door.

"Oh, hell no!" I leapt from behind the boulder, sprinting the short distance to the door. The orange pulses came closer and I looked up to see a laser strike the boulder where Markus had been hiding. It exploded, sending rock fragments flying in all directions. Crap. I didn't want to see what it would do to me. Reluctant to switch the gun to my other hand, I grasped the door handle with my injured one, grateful for the protective glove I wore this time. Rapid footsteps pounded behind me as I yanked it open.

I tried to scramble inside and close the door, but hands were on my back, pushing me down the ladder. The laser pulses sounded like they were almost on top of us. My foot caught on the bottom rung and I tumbled in an awkward somersault. Footsteps crashed down the ladder above me while I struggled to regain my bearings. Three figures stood a few feet away. A fourth figure pulled the heavy door closed as a barrage of light pulses rained down on it.

"Graceful as ever, Tora." Markus stood across from me. He tore off his helmet and then placed his gun back in the holster.

Keeping hold of my gun, I used my other hand to remove my helmet. Sweat poured down my neck and frizzy, dark ringlets fell over my eyes. I tossed my head back, trying to keep my line of sight clear. Staring upward, I realized what a genius my father had been. He must have known the lasers wouldn't affect this type of metal. He'd constructed a bomb shelter, not just a keep-away-the-sun-shelter. Though the lasers had pulverized the boulder, the door held tight.

Markus shrugged and had the nerve to smirk at me. "Guess we're all on the same side now."

Chapter SIX

THE DAY MY MOTHER AND SISTER DIED, I'D MADE A BARGAIN. They'd only been gone a short time, but had left their suits behind, and in this climate, every second counted. My father went to look for them and ordered me to stay put. I wasn't even sure who I was bargaining with; any god with half a brain would have fled this hellhole long ago. But I wanted my family safe. Speaking to the empty air, I'd promised that if my mother and sister were alive, I would spend the rest of my days being more helpful and less of a smart-ass. I'd be a better person. A minute later, my father found them. They weren't even remotely close to alive. All bets were off.

I leveled my gun at Markus. "I will never be on 'your side.' Get out."

Loud humming filled the room. The three suits had their guns aimed at me with their fingers on the engagement triggers.

"Settle down, sweetie." Markus turned to the group. "No one's going to shoot anyone. Let's calm ourselves."

"If you kill me now, you'll never get the guns. Right, Markus? Except that didn't seem to bother you earlier when you were all shooting at me."

He laughed. "I already told you . . . we were trying to incapacitate you, not kill you. Besides, you can't kill us either—I doubt you'll escape the Consulate lackeys out there on your own."

I flashed him a withering look. Of course they wanted me alive; Markus must have told them only I could fire the guns. If it prevented the Consulate from killing me outright, maybe it wasn't such a bad thing. "I was doing just fine before you all came along. And they didn't seem to be shooting at me."

The largest of the suits spoke. It was the deep voice from earlier who'd asked to check on his dead guy. "Look, we're all in the same situation here. See, I'm putting my gun down." He turned off the trigger and placed the gun at his feet. He reached up and slowly removed his helmet. His short hair was drenched in sweat.

The smaller of the other two suits—it had to be the girl—yanked off her helmet. "It's too frickin' hot for this shit. Would someone please tell me what the hell is going on out there? Aren't they supposed to be on our side, Kale?"

She was small, dark, and bony. Even her cheeks looked sharp—like those mean-looking birds I'd once come across on the GlobalNet. I'd been glad they'd died out before I came along. She lowered her gun, but didn't drop it.

I glanced over at Markus, annoyed at the amusement on his face. Bad choice on my part. The humming sound warned me just in time, and I dove to the floor and rolled. The laser hit the wall behind me and created a shower of sparks. I came up, my weapon aimed at the girl who'd just fired at me, but the tall man, Kale, had already knocked her gun out of her hands.

"That's enough," he boomed. "You never shoot without an order. Got it, soldier?"

The girl glared at me. She kicked the floor with her boot. "Got it," she mumbled.

My relief lasted only for the second it took for him to hand the gun back to her. "Next time I take your gun, it's for good."

The girl grunted in reply. It seemed clear that Kale was in charge, or was supposed to be anyway. He looked older than Markus by a good decade. My pulse wouldn't stop racing, and I stood slowly, not lowering my gun. Had Kale putting his gun down been a trick? Did they think I was completely stupid?

That was when the third suit, which either had to be a guy or quite a strapping young lady, put down his gun in a halting way, as if reluctant to let go of it. He took off his helmet and laid it carefully by his weapon.

I sucked in my breath when he looked directly at me. The guy had an intense stare. His sandy blond hair matched the scruff on his face, and he didn't look much older than me—I'd say three years max. He might even be considered sort of cute if I didn't count the whole killer-for-hire thing against him. Which I did. Of course, maybe he only seemed cute because, before today, I could count the number of boys I'd seen in the past year on one finger. His eyes held mine for an instant before he turned to the older man. He didn't say a word, just eyed him with a questioning expression.

Kale sighed. "One of my contacts must have gone to the Consulate after we left Caelia. Sold me out for some currency."

I frowned, confused. "What are you talking about? Didn't the Consulate hire you?"

Scruffy boy chimed in. "They probably figured out he wasn't going to hand the guns over." His voice sounded deep and rough, like his vocal cords had been rubbed with sandpaper. I wanted him to say more but he didn't. Why hadn't Kale planned to hand over the guns? It wasn't like any greater payment than a UCC existed.

Markus whirled to face Kale. "What? You wanted to double-cross the Consulate? Well, I want my UCC." He punched the table with his fist. "I never would have agreed to this if I'd known about this bullshit."

"Exactly," said Kale. "And we needed you in case Tora needed some extra persuasion. Don't get your panties in a bunch. I planned to pay you myself for your services." He gestured above us. "But first we need a way out of here."

Markus glanced at the girl. "Were you in on this too, Britta?"

Somehow the name fit her. Britta just shrugged.

I laughed at Markus. "Aw, you poor thing . . . doesn't feel good to be screwed over, does it? Well, now the Consulate knows where the guns are and don't need any of your sorry asses. There's no way they'll let you live now."

Britta whined. "I didn't sign up for this. I just want my money and I want to go home." She glared at me with her beady black eyes. Britta the bird. "But first, I really want to be the one to hurt her."

"I don't think anyone's going home anytime soon, Britta," Kale said. "And there will be no hurting anyone tonight."

I noticed the "tonight" qualifier. Should I be grateful they wouldn't maim me until morning? Maybe I should let them know that my finger wouldn't work on the weapons security door if I was dead.

The aerial attack continued a bit longer above us, and then came to an abrupt halt. Maybe it dawned on them that I could easily take them down with one of my father's super-guns. Or they were just changing strategies.

Britta grumbled as she peeled off her suit. "I still don't get why the government would kill their own?"

I yawned in mock boredom. "They must not see you as valuable. You're certainly not a very good shot." I eyed bird girl and scruffy boy. "Let me guess—you're two of Earth's last juvenile delinquents. You already got in trouble on Caelia and this mission was your chance at redeeming yourselves. Sorry it didn't work out so well."

Britta lunged at me, barely held back by Kale.

Scruffy boy shot icicles at me with his eyes. "You don't know anything about me."

"Give it a rest, Tora," said Markus. "We're all tired here."

He sounded eerily like Dad, who used to ride me for my "relentless sarcasm." My mother defended it, saying it made me a fighter and that it was "better to have dark humor than none." She'd said once that if she'd had some of my spunk, she might not have needed so many meds.

Kale shifted and cleared his throat. "Um, Tora, can I use the bathroom?"

I suppressed my laughter. Their fearless leader went from trying to shoot me to requesting to take a piss. It's amazing the difference an hour can make in one's life. I pointed to a small door off to the side and snorted. "Make sure you aim into the center of the machine—we recycle here."

A container in the room collected and sterilized urine before running it through a tube in the wall back to the W.A.R. unit. Even though it tasted like water again once it was recycled, drinking my own piss was one thing—I cringed at the thought of drinking theirs. I kept my gun lowered but refused to let my guard down, trying to remember if there was anything in the bathroom Kale could use against me. *Not unless he gets really creative with the waterless toothpaste.* My shoulders relaxed a little when he came out empty-handed.

"Let's all take a load off and sort this out," said Markus, gesturing to the empty seats around him. He sounded genial but I caught the suspicious look he sent Kale's way. Maybe Kale screwing him over could benefit me. I had a shortage of allies at the moment and could use someone on my side—even Markus.

Markus parked himself in Dad's chair. I still couldn't bring myself to sit in the ones that my mom and sister used. Let them sit. I'd stand. I waved my arm toward the table in mock hospitality.

The group jostled cautiously around me, joining Markus. Kale nodded at me as he moved past while scruffy boy averted his eyes, looking at some invisible spot on the floor. But not bird girl. No, Britta gave me a silent bitch slap with her eyes as she sat.

Tomblike silence filled the room, but the quiet from above was more disconcerting.

"Maybe they gave up?" Britta asked Kale.

"Not a chance. I think they're rethinking their strategy."

Markus frowned. "Or maybe they'll cut the air line— not that it worked last time."

I froze. I thought back to Markus' first visit but was positive I hadn't mentioned it. "How did you know the line was cut before?"

Markus looked sheepish, and seemed to weigh his options before giving his traditional shrug. "Look, I thought it would hurry your decision a bit if I made a tiny dent in the line. If you couldn't fix it, you'd have to come with me."

I slammed my hand against the wall. "And I'd have to give you my guns. You are such an asshole."

Britta stared at the door above, ignoring my outburst. "Do you think they have other weapons? Something that could blast this place open?" She looked terrified and almost childlike. I would have felt sorry for her if she were someone else.

Kale glanced at me before answering. "No, they don't have a weapon that powerful."

"But she does," Markus said, jerking his thumb at me. Could he be any more of a burner? "Which is why they want them so badly."

"They?" I couldn't help myself. "It's why you want them so badly too—so you can make a buck."

"I'm a simple businessman," said Markus. "A guy's gotta eat."

"And drink," added Britta. "Speaking of which, I'm dying of thirst. All our water's on the ship."

I checked the level on the W.A.R. and my stomach dropped. Even if we divided it five ways we'd have less than a quarter cup each. For the entire day. After being outside for several hours, I could chug two gallons in minutes, and the others had been out there longer than me. Not that I planned to share. Even if everyone used the special piss machine, it wouldn't make much difference. Sure, I could try to kill them all and keep the water for myself, but that wouldn't make me any better than them. As it stood, we didn't need to worry about shooting each other because we'd die of dehydration first.

Water, the great equalizer.

Maybe the government figured this out. Maybe that's why they halted the air strike. They realized we'd eventually come out begging for mercy—and water. They didn't need to attack. They could just wait.

Chapter SEVEN

THE CONTINUED QUIET ABOVE SEEMED MORE MENACING THAN the assault had been. Everyone lapped up their measly water rations in seconds. I didn't know it was possible to be so thirsty. My mouth still tasted like ash, my tongue thick and heavy. I had my reasons for sharing, mainly to gain their trust and make it look like I was a team player. In reality, I wanted to punch every one of them, but that would only make me thirstier.

We sat and eyed each other warily. The way Britta kept looking at me, I knew she saw an extra inch of water where my head should be. I wondered how long it would be before she'd try to take me out again.

"Any ideas on the H_2O situation?" Markus asked, tapping the butt of his gun on the table.

"We've got plenty of water on the ship. Or had anyway," said Kale. "They might have gone aboard her by now, although I don't know if they'd have thought to take the water. There's so much water on Caelia, people are already forgetting how scarce it was here."

Britta scoffed. "Like we could make it to the ship anyway. They'd torch us as soon as we got outside this door."

Scruffy boy remained silent as usual, not looking at anyone in particular. For some reason, this was getting under my skin. "Are you always this mute?"

He gazed right at me, responding calmly. "Unless I have something to say."

I glared back at him. "We could die here and you've got nothing to contribute?"

He looked away, which only infuriated me more. After a minute of silence, he cleared his throat and looked to Kale. "What about at night? We might have a shot of making it then if we can stay out of sight . . . and survive the night storms."

I jumped in before Kale could respond. "Wow . . . two whole sentences. You're making progress." I knew I was being a bitch—guess living in an isolated environment for most of my life hadn't done wonders for my social skills. "Also, I hate to be a negative Nellie, but going out at night is suicide. There is no surviving the night storms . . . the winds would shred us alive."

His hazel eyes glared into mine before he looked away again.

"You're as sweet as ever, Tora. And you wonder why I left you here." Markus wore a smug expression. I really wanted to knock it off him. "Besides, we might be able to make it at night . . . if we go really, really fast."

Kale drummed his fingers on the table. "Good idea, James. That might be our best shot."

James. Scruffy sort-of-cute boy was James. It was a total downer that the cutest boy I'd seen in my short life had tried to kill me. I stared at him, then tightened my grip on the gun.

Kale did most of the talking; Britta did most of the whining. Markus tried to catch my eye a few times, but I refused to look at him. I was too mad about the air line to want him on my side at the moment. James threw in an occasional comment or question but otherwise kept silent, watching everyone. Including me. I stayed ten feet back from the table, waiting to see how their plans included me so I could then tell them to go to hell. It was their ship over the horizon, not mine. Let them go out and get killed by the Consulate. What did I care?

James looked up and our eyes met. My stomach fluttered in a way it hadn't before. Apparently I did care. I made a mental note to ignore my stomach.

"If they kill us out there, they'll come for you next. They won't kill you, but they won't stop until they have the guns." James continued to stare at me, which caused my stomach to go all weird again. "Your weapons are powerful, but it's not like one person can use them all at once."

I'd only need one weapon if I used my very special one, not that I'd tell him that.

I thought about all the time my father had invested in my weapons training—though I'd never even used the deadliest one of all. Getting the guns here in the first place had taken some doing. He'd had a crew of similar-minded antigovernment folks bring in the materials and help him construct the bunker, far from the prying eyes of the Consulate. Due to the amount of help he had, it took just a few months. We continued living at our house in the pod city, so the Consulate never knew what my dad was up to. He showed up at work every day, perfecting the guns, only traveling to our shelter-in-progress on the weekends. He had to get the guns to a secret location before the specified delivery date.

Luckily for us, people were dropping like flies at that point. The state of the global emergency, which grew exponentially worse with each passing month, had distracted the leaders from the fact that my father's promised weapons had vanished from under their noses. Yet now, they knew exactly where they were. They'd never stop. James was right that I couldn't take them all out with one regular gun, but T.O. would do the trick. I shook the thought away. T.O. would take everyone out—except me.

"Wouldn't it be easier if we just gave Tora over to them? Maybe they'd let us go," Britta asked, disappointment in her voice. Britta the bitch. So many possible nicknames to choose from.

Kale shook his head impatiently. "No, she stays. What is it you're suggesting, James?"

James looked steadily at Kale. "I'm suggesting she come with us."

Hell, no. But I bit my tongue and hoped he'd elaborate.

"Are you kidding me?" Britta wailed.

"James never kids," said Kale, still tapping his fingers.

Markus shot me a hopeful look, like he suddenly cared what happened to me. I ignored him.

Kale acted as if a sudden revelation dawned on him. "Ah yes, the safety in numbers thing. If something happened to us, you'd be here alone. You against the Consulate."

I wanted to laugh. Being alone meant I could lock their lame asses out of the bunker and be done with them. Their attempt at pretending to care about my well-being was insulting. I knew exactly what they were thinking. That since I was the one with the super-guns, and the only one who could fire them, their odds of getting their water were much better with me than without me. No way was I getting those guns out of the safe.

However, as much as I wanted this fun little group out of my house, the thought of them dying out there and leaving me to fend off the government myself was not the smartest option. I'd have no way off the planet. Maybe Britta dying would be okay, but the thought of Markus dying didn't sit right with me—though it probably should have. None of that mattered now anyway, because what I really, really wanted was to get my hands on some water.

The signs of early dehydration were already kicking in and I could almost taste the water on his ship.

I glanced at James, whose gaze had returned to me. "I'm in."

Markus' eyebrows raised in surprise. No doubt he'd been expecting a sarcastic tirade from me, telling them all to burn in hell.

"But I expect to get a cut of your water. And any other supplies you bring back."

Markus smirked. "There's the girl I know. You had me worried there for a minute."

I had to stop myself from smiling—doing things just for my own personal gain was very Markus-like. No wonder he approved.

Britta stomped her foot on the floor, like a three-year-old who had just been told she couldn't have a second glass of water. "No way in hell is she getting a drop of my H_2O!" She turned to Kale, the angular side of her nose looking somehow more beaklike. "Tell her, Kale!"

Kale exhaled deeply. "Calm down, Brit."

Oh, a new one. Brit the twit.

"But it's not fair—"

"Oh, for Caesar's sake, I do believe that's her water you drank there," Kale said, tilting his head toward the empty cup in front of Britta. "She helps us get there, she gets water. Simple as that."

Britta crossed her arms in front of her, glaring down at the table.

Oh, no, not the silent treatment. Anything but that. Maybe if I played my cards right, she'd be quiet forever.

Kale stretched. "We should probably try to get a little rest before nightfall."

I thought of the small labyrinth of rooms surrounding us. My door had a lock, so I wasn't worried about someone breaking in, and there was no way anyone was sharing my room with me. My room. It was actually my parents' room, but after my father died, I moved in. I couldn't stand the reminder of my sister's death every night—her empty sleep pad taunting me from across our shared room. Plus, my parents' room was the one closest to this front room. And closest to the exit. The sleep-chamber-for-two size was a bonus.

"Everyone walk that way. I'll be right behind you." No way was I going to walk in front of four people who just tried to kill me. Or incapacitate me. Whatever. "Oh, and all your guns stay with me."

I swear I saw James' mouth twitch. Did he find this amusing?

"No way in hell is she taking my gun. Who does she think she is?" Britta's silent treatment didn't last nearly as long as I would have liked.

"It'll be fine. I know her. She's not going to hurt us." Markus went to his gun and tossed it across the floor to me, like it was no big deal. His eyes met mine and I gave him a short nod of gratitude. That's all I was giving him.

"We'll need these back tonight, you understand?" Kale asked.

"No problem. But there's no reason to have them in here." I flashed a smile at Britta as I scooped up the three other guns that Kale slid over. "Since when is it considered polite for houseguests to be armed?"

Britta looked like she was going to implode. "Then you need to get rid of yours too."

I raised my laser and pointed it right between Britta's eyes. Her startled gasp made me want to laugh. "Get this straight, little girl. I don't need to do anything. I could take you all out right now." I waved my finger over the pulsing blue square. "But I'm not going to do that because I have a semblance of a moral code." My gaze fell on Markus. "Unlike you all."

I gestured around me with Trigger, still holding their guns in my other arm. "This obviously is the kitchen and energy packets are locked in the cabinet there." I wiggled my thumb at them. "And I'm the only one that can open it. Same with the button that operates the W.A.R., so you can forget about sneaking water." Not that there was any to sneak. The container was dry as dirt.

I gestured for them to move down the hallway ahead of me. My room was the first on the right. I stopped and placed my thumb on the red square in the door. An audible click preceded my door swinging open, and I tossed their guns inside before locking it again.

"I couldn't help noticing the double-sized chamber in there, Tora. I'm willing to share with you, if it'll help."

"In your dreams, Markus. Keep moving."

Across from my room was the sole lavatory. Aside from the small unit that evacuated waste, there was a small cabinet filled with waterless soap for washing clothes—and bodies. Thinking of how much sweating I'd done in the last few hours and how fantastic I must smell, I couldn't wait to steal a few moments in there. An energetic wand, called eTeeth, used high-frequency vibrations to eradicate plaque and bacteria from your mouth. I'd have to hide that in my room. I didn't want my wand in anyone else's mouth.

"The bathroom lock is the only generic one in this place. It's triggered by any thumbprint. All the others were keyed to our individual thumbprints, so you can't lock—or unlock—anything else in here."

Next to the lavatory, farther down the hall, was a small study. It was intended as a place for my father to continue his work. Not his weaponry work, but his work in the antigovernment movement. It was a small space containing his writing station, a stack of thermoplastic-fiber notebooks, and a padded bench. The furniture had been brought in from the pod city. It wasn't much, but it was my favorite room in this godforsaken place. After his death, I would lie on the bench either watching old videos or reading archived books on the Infinity, escaping to different worlds for hours at a time. I could make the three-dimensional screen as large as I wanted, so, at times, I literally surrounded myself in words. It was the closest I felt to happy.

I looked back at the room. "Someone could have the bench in here, I guess." I hated that someone else might have my favorite space. "But the couch up front is probably more comfortable than this."

We turned the corner and continued down the narrow corridor. My old room, the one I'd shared with my sister, came next, about halfway down the hall. It contained two twin sleep pads. Mine had been the one closest to the door, like I could better protect my sister that way. I had no idea what I might be protecting her from, but I'd foolishly thought she was safer with me as the first line of defense. There's no defense against Mother Nature—she's one fatal bitch.

I stared at the group. They didn't deserve to sleep where she did. But they sure as hell weren't sleeping with me. I sighed. "Two of you could sleep in here."

"Great. Guess I'm stuck with one of you, since James needs his space, and I'm not about to sleep on the couch out in the open," said Britta to Markus. She glared at me like I had developed a master plan to kill her while she slept.

Kale nodded at them. "You two take this room, James can have his space, and I'll take the couch."

James needed his space? What did that mean? Maybe he and Britta had been an item and now he wanted to get away from her. If that was the case, he had some serious bad taste in girlfriends.

Across from this room was a small recreation room, with a motion machine and several other pieces of equipment. My father deemed it important to stay healthy since we had no access to medical care aside from our first-aid kit. His long-term plan involved our relocation to a magical new planet—I think he overestimated the chances of finding one just as much as he overestimated Markus. In the meantime, Dad said forty-five minutes of exercise per day was optimal, so that's what I did. I didn't do a second less, but I didn't do more either. And in truth, my activity on the motion machine was more what I would call creative walking than running. I didn't see the point of running if someone wasn't chasing me.

The hall ended at a small closet. I didn't want them to get suspicious, so I took them there. It contained assorted blankets, linens, and towels—all made from a variety of the plastic fibers that everything else in our world was made of. If the inventor of heat-resistant thermoplastics had survived, they'd be a bazillionaire. "Extra bedding if you need it. Nothing exciting."

They couldn't see the small lock on the back wall of the closet. It opened up into a large room. "The room of lethal weapons" as I called it. I shut the closet door and turned to the group. "And this concludes our guided tour for today. If you'll excuse me, I'm going to get some sleep."

I started to move down the hallway when Markus cleared his throat. "Seriously, Tora, I'd like to keep you company. You must be lonely having spent all this time without people around."

He sounded shockingly sincere. I didn't respond to him or even acknowledge him as I headed to my room. When safely inside, I pressed my thumb against the square to lock the door and exhaled, my head leaning against the door. I climbed onto my sleep pad and curled up. Markus was right, in a way. But it wasn't about being lonely. Despite being surrounded by more people than I'd seen in years, I'd never felt more alone.

Chapter EIGHT

A WHIRRING SOUND INTERRUPTED MY DREAMS AND I SAT UP with a start, rubbing the sleep from my eyes. Although there were no windows, I knew it was night without even glancing at the clock. No one had knocked on my door. Maybe they left to retrieve their water without me. Maybe they decided to try their luck and run for it, see if their ship could outrun the government ones. I jumped down, powered up my gun, then pressed my ear to the door but heard nothing except the faint noise.

I tucked a stray piece of hair behind my ear and pushed my thumb to the lock. The soft click sounded loud to me, but after a minute, I moved into the hallway. Kale snored loudly from the couch, but the front room was otherwise empty and so was the bathroom. As I moved slowly down the hallway, the whirring sound grew louder. Turning to my left, I noticed the empty study. Had James changed his mind about needing space?

As I got closer, I recognized the sound. The motion machine. So that's what it sounded like when someone actually ran on it. Someone had decided that extra exercise was more fun than sleeping. I knew these burners were crazy. To my right, I heard someone grunting in their sleep. Markus. The room looked dark underneath the door. At least one of them was sleeping. I reached the half-closed door to the recreation room.

I peered through the small opening in the door and saw James. James with his shirt off, running as if an army of rabid soldiers was chasing him. His body was solid muscle. Sweat dripped down his face, his chest, his arms . . . he wasn't just sort of cute, he was hot. My gun bumped against the door and it swung open. James' head jerked toward the door, where I leaned in an obvious spy pose. Blood rushed to my face.

He pressed a button, turning off the power to the machine. "Sorry, I thought I'd get a run in before tonight. Did you want to use it?" Although he looked like he'd been running for hours, he barely sounded winded.

I stood up, trying to regain my composure. "No thanks. Holding on to rocks in gale force winds is enough exercise for the day in my book."

A hint of a smile crossed his face, which caused that strange fluttering sensation again in my stomach. Ignoring it, I pressed him. "Didn't you sleep at all? Aren't you tired?"

"Nah, I don't get tired. And yes, I did sleep . . . a little." Sweat continued to run down his body, a body I was trying very hard not to look at. He grabbed a towel he must've found in the linen closet, and rubbed the sweat from his face and hair.

He was just a guy, like Markus, so why couldn't I seem to take my eyes off him? It's not like I had any trouble keeping them off Markus. James stopped wiping himself and stood there, watching me watch him.

He smiled and stepped closer. "What about you? Sleep well?"

I racked my brain for a flippant remark but came up blank. Where was my sarcasm when I needed it most? My heart thudded like crazy. *Walk away from him, now.* My body wasn't listening to me. "Uh, I guess."

James eyed me as he ran the towel through his hair a final time. He took another step toward me and spoke in a low voice. "Look, I know it might not seem it, but I'm not one of the bad guys."

"Then I'd hate to see what the good guys are like." My trusty defense mechanism had kicked back in just in time. I'd been in danger of letting my guard down and actually talking to the guy.

Kale's booming voice startled me. "Well, it's about that time. You two ready?" I'd been so busy trying to tear my eyes away from James that I hadn't heard Kale come down the hall.

"Yes, sir." James walked toward me, and I felt frozen in place. He touched my arm lightly, and I inhaled the scent of his sweat. It reminded me of the ocean. Or at least like the smell of the digital ocean I'd spent hours of my life enveloped in. "You ready?"

"Yes," I answered. I fought a strange urge to touch a drop of sweat rolling down his neck. Get ahold of yourself. I guess not being around boys much explained the attraction, but how could I think someone was hot at a time like this? *Just because the world is ending doesn't mean you're blind.*

Britta complained she'd barely slept but kept throwing coy glances at Markus. Oh, good God, no way. He must have worked his magic on yet another female survivor.

We made our way up to the front room, as Markus stretched and yawned. He touched Britta's arm with a sly smile on his face. They apparently had quite the night. Remembering my promise, I stopped in my room to get their guns. While donning our suits, Kale went over the basic points of the plan. The only part that really caught my attention was when he said I'd be with James. Britta and Markus would be paired—now there was a match made in heaven. Kale would go first and provide cover for us.

"What about her weapons?" Britta asked.

Um, did she not understand the part where I said I wasn't giving over the guns?

Kale shook his head. "My ship is too far and I'm guessing the weapons would weigh us down." He looked at me. "Are there a lot?"

I nodded. He had no idea.

"We'll be lucky to make it as it is," Kale said.

"But—"

"Enough, Britta." Kale didn't leave room for more commentary.

It made me glad his ship wasn't close or I'm sure they would have overpowered me in order to take the guns.

I grabbed my helmet. Even though we wouldn't be fighting sun glare at night, the oxygen levels weren't great and we'd need the extra oxygen in our suits if we had to run—which I'm guessing we would. Also, they would shield us from the weather. The nights were as cold as the days were hot, and the sturdy helmets would provide some protection from flying debris. With this thought, I noticed the howling of the wind outside. "I hate to point out the obvious," I said. "But how exactly are we supposed to get through this night storm?"

James looked calm as he answered. "We wait for it to end and run for it. And hope we get to the ship before the next one starts."

The look on Britta's face was of pure horror. I'd wager this whole mission was a tad more than she bargained for.

"Look at the bright side," added Kale. "There's no way their ship is out flying in this storm. It would get torn apart. They'd likely find a valley or someplace safer to wait through the night."

Markus laughed as he zipped up his suit, the zipper

seam instantly disappearing into the fabric when he finished. "Yeah, it's not like they'd think we'd be freakin' crazy enough to run for the ship at night."

He was right about one thing. We were crazy to try this. It's amazing what one would do for water. Speaking of, only inches of it had accumulated in the W.A.R. machine in the last few hours. "Wait!"

Everyone stared at me. I ran to grab the cups from the table. "We should drink what we can before we leave. Who knows what will happen out there?"

Markus eyed me with suspicion as I handed him his tiny ration. He even sniffed it first, which made me chuckle. "You can't blame me, Tora. Your sudden generosity is a little surprising."

Maybe I was getting used to having company around, no matter how dysfunctional they were.

I felt James watching me, and my cheeks grew warm. He rested his empty cup on the table. "Thanks, Tora."

I met his gaze briefly, then dropped my eyes, embarrassed that he could somehow see the effect he had on me.

The raging winds subsided above us. Silence filled the air. Kale grabbed his helmet. "Okay, this is our window. Is everyone good to go? Use the com system in the helmets to communicate—I don't want you taking off your helmet unless it's an emergency. Got it?"

The others nodded. James walked over to me, my helmet in his hand. He held it out to me. "Here."

"Thanks." His fingers brushed mine as he handed it to

me and an electric charge ran up my arm. I blushed.

Kale studied me a second, then put his helmet on. I'd go along with the plan but he wasn't my commander and I sure as hell wasn't taking orders from him. I put on my helmet. The others headed up the ladder behind Kale, and I followed. After everyone was outside, I shut the door behind me.

We stood in the darkness, the moon nothing but a dim spot in the distance. No sight of the huge Consulate ship. A slight breeze stirred the air, reminding me that our time was short. It was also damn cold. I jumped up and down, trying to keep warm. Kale ran to the rock he'd hidden behind when they first attacked me. After checking to make sure it was clear, he motioned us onward then took off again toward the next rock. "All clear," he said.

I jumped at the sound of his voice in my helmet. Markus and Britta went next, while James and I brought up the rear. I made sure to keep clear of the cactus grove. The blue light panel of my gun glowed reassuringly in the dark, though I hoped I wouldn't have to use it. It was ironic that Trigger was the closest thing I had to a pet, but I never wanted to use it for its intended purpose.

Running alongside James, I realized he had to be slowing his pace for my sake. We'd gone maybe a hundred yards and I was already breathless. My forty-five minutes a day on the motion machine were clearly no match for his kamikaze workout routine. Maybe I should have done more jogging and less walking after all.

"You okay?" James' voice penetrated my ear, his husky words burning into me through the com system.

"Yeah, I'm okay," I managed between gasps. At least there was no wind, so I didn't have to worry as much about inhaling dust on top of my pathetic sprinting skills. Kale glanced over his shoulder to check on us.

Kale's ship remained out of sight, over the ridge, about five hundred more yards away. Running there and back was going to count as my exercise for the entire week. Still no sign of the Consulate ship. Markus was right. They wouldn't think we'd be nuts enough to go outside at night. They were probably bunkered down enjoying a good night's sleep, certain we'd come out waving a white flag in the morning.

Another two hundred yards and I was panting harder than I had in my life. Making matters worse, the cold penetrated every fiber of my being and my toes were numb. The night had grown almost pitch-black, the light provided by the moon, minuscule. My feet pounded the ground, twisting a few times as I stepped on several small rocks.

The sound of my own breathing, loud and erratic, filled my helmet, punctuated by the occasional expletive from Markus. I noticed Markus had slowed his pace as well. He'd never struck me as much of an exercising kind of guy. At least I might be able to outrun him if necessary, though I could never outrun James or Kale.

We'd almost reached the ridge and aside from my bruised ribs screaming at me, things were looking pretty good. We were almost there. The night didn't seem quite so scary after all.

I didn't notice at first. I'd been breathing so hard, I didn't hear it. It wasn't until a rock skittered across my foot that the whooshing of the wind registered. James was a short step ahead of me, and he turned, tugging on my sleeve to hurry up. I heard Britta's panicked shrieking in my ear. "Run!"

I cranked my legs, trying to move faster, but they burned in protest, practically shouting that they were doing the best they could. They felt like rubber append-ages beneath my torso. My lungs were on fire, the icy cold air like a vise clamping around them. A rock hit my calf as the gusts grew stronger. Unfortunately, this last stretch contained no large boulders—nothing to hold on to when things got worse. Which they would. Very soon.

Finally Kale's ship came into view, maybe a hundred yards away. Crap, it was so freaking cold outside that a hundred yards seemed like a mile. The wind whistled through my helmet, almost rhythmic in its deadly hum. *Please let me make it.* James dropped back and placed his hand behind my arm, propelling my numb body onward. He yelled something that sounded like "hurry," but I couldn't hear him clearly over the howling of the wind.

Another gust ripped through the air and my feet lifted briefly off the ground. Only James' firm hold of my arm kept me anchored to Earth.

Kale made it to his ship and the hatch door opened. My

eyes fixed on that door; it beckoned yet mocked me with its distance. Thirty yards away. A bowling-ball-sized rock flew past, narrowly missing my head. Britta and Markus rushed through the ship's door. The air around me screamed.

Fifteen yards. Almost there. A second later, my feet weren't touching the ground. James literally pulled me through the air toward the door. Markus and Britta stood in the entrance, making desperate motions with their arms. Their screams mixed with the shrieking winds in my ears. They moved back as Kale gripped the door frame with one hand and reached out to James to pull us inside. The safe haven of that doorway was a few feet away.

It came out of nowhere—something sharp in my side that hurt like hell. I felt blood running down the inside of my suit. Then everything went black.

Chapter NINE

MY FATHER SPOKE TO ME TENDERLY THE NIGHT BEFORE HIS murder. Part of him must have suspected his Consulate visit was a one-way trip. He'd gone over all the safety procedures because he said this business trip might be longer than usual. I hadn't guessed then just how long my alone time would be. For the first time, he hadn't had me practice with the guns after dinner. He said he hoped I'd never need to touch them again. Then he kissed me good night, which he hadn't done since the night he found my mother and sister dead.

The voice filtering through my mind at the moment was not tender. It sounded grating and harsh.

"Could someone please explain why we're helping her? She only came so she could take part of the water anyway, so why are we giving a crap?"

"You're almost as much of a charmer as Tora."

I didn't need to open my eyes to picture that beaklike nose. I tried opening them anyway, and squinted in the intense light of the room. Markus stood near Britta, watching me with amusement. I tried to sit up but fell back in pain.

Markus chuckled. "Somebody took a hard hit."

I gritted my teeth. "From what?" I twisted around as if the mysterious cause of my injury would be found somewhere in the room. Dizziness overtook me and everything blurred. It took a minute for my vision to clear.

James sat in a chair behind me. His head leaned back against the wall like he was too tired to hold it upright. His eyes drooped in apparent fatigue. "A rock. Two of your ribs are fractured."

I touched my left side under the white medical gown, and could feel bandages covering the area. *Medical gown? Where the hell are my clothes?*

"How did I get in this?" I asked, picking up the hem of the gown.

"I sure as hell didn't help you," said Britta. She flung her straight hair over her shoulder. "I'd better go tell our leader that the princess is awake." Britta stormed to the door, then turned to Markus and raised an eyebrow at him. "Coming?"

I glared at Markus. He smirked. "Don't look at me. Ask the medic there." He gestured at James, then followed after Britta down the hall.

Blood flooded my cheeks. Aside from my panties, the only things under this flimsy excuse of a gown were bandages. It took everything I had to turn and face him again and, even then, I couldn't meet his eyes. "You put me in this gown?"

When he responded with silence, I was forced to look up. I swallowed, trying to sound nonchalant. "Aren't you a little young to be the ship's medic?"

"It's what I trained to do, before some other stuff happened."

I should have trained to be a dentist, because getting more than a sentence out of him at a time was like pulling teeth. "And?"

At least he had the decency to look embarrassed. "I'm sorry. I needed to check your ribs and clean up the wound before I taped it."

"Please tell me Markus wasn't in here." I knew Markus best, yet he was the last person I would want to see me naked.

"No. No one was. I tried to get Britta to help . . . "

I put up my hand to stop him. "No explanation needed there." I eased off the metal bed, but the dizziness returned and I stumbled.

"Whoa." James rushed to my side, easing his arm around my waist. "Easy there." He guided me back onto the bed into a sitting position.

My head pounded and my vision went out of whack.

I tried hard to bring James into focus. "What's wrong with me?"

His arm stayed around me, keeping me steady. "Do you mean medically—or otherwise?"

I heard the smile in his voice and relaxed. "You're lucky I can't see you well, or I'd smack you."

His tone grew serious. "Mild concussion. You flew out of my grasp when the rock hit you, and you hit your head pretty hard on a step of the ship. You should be fine in a few days though. The ribs will take longer to heal." He cleared his throat and turned me to face him. "I'm sorry I couldn't hold on."

Though still dizzy and nauseous, the concern and remorse on his face were unmistakable. I had a strange urge to reach out and touch the blond stubble on his chin. Though I still didn't trust him, he had saved me when he could have let me die. "I wouldn't have made it at all if it wasn't for you. Thank you."

We stared at each other until I heard footsteps in the hallway.

"See? She's just fine. I don't see what all the fuss was about," Britta said, hand on her hip.

I pulled my eyes away from James. I couldn't afford to get attached to anyone anyway. After all I'd lost, I'd learned it was better not to care.

Markus touched Britta's arm and her stance softened a little. She flashed Markus a tiny smile. They'd apparently done some serious bonding during their night together. I shook my head—that was a visual I didn't need right now.

"What do you say, James?" asked Kale.

"Sir, her ribs will take time to heal and her head will be hurting for a bit, but I think she'll be fine. Her suit repaired itself adequately."

"Nice work," said Kale. "Tora, we'll leave you here to rest while we gather up some supplies. We can't go back until the storm ends."

It must still be night. I couldn't hear any bombs going off in the distance, just the unmistakable winds. I noted a container of water by my bed, with a Caelia Pure label on it. Real water from another planet, not the recycled piss I'd been drinking forever. James nodded at me and I chugged the whole thing in three gulps. This must be what heaven tastes like. I couldn't believe they had bottles and bottles of the stuff. We could drink water whenever we were thirsty.

"Why can't we just take off and run for it?" Britta asked. "It'll be light in less than an hour and they'll be back."

"No," said Kale.

He didn't say anything else. He didn't need to. I knew he wouldn't leave without the guns. They were his only bargaining chip. But we did need to get back to the bunker before daylight or the Consulate would be waiting for us.

"We need to go," I said, realizing how improbable it sounded. Between my concussion and cracked ribs, I'd never move fast enough to make it home between the storms.

"Astute observation there, my dear," said Markus. "Wanna tell us how we can do that?"

"Yeah," answered James. Every head in the room turned to him. One of the perks of not saying much was that everyone paid attention when he did. "We fly there."

"Huh?" asked Britta. "You mean like fly a hundred feet?"

Kale looked at Britta like she wasn't the brightest bulb in the bunch. "More like eighteen hundred feet." He turned to James. "Brilliant plan." Which it was. I wondered why James wasn't in charge of this ragtag group.

"The Consulate could destroy the ship once it's parked there," James noted.

Kale stroked his chin. "Maybe, but I think it'd be more useful to them whole—or for parts. They'd be crazy not to want a second space drive. We'll kill them before that happens."

A tiny voice nagged in my head saying that maybe James wasn't just trying to spare me from the night storms. Maybe it was part tactical reasoning. Kale wanted the guns and like he'd said earlier, it wasn't practical to transfer the guns when the ship was so far from the shelter. It would certainly be easier if his ship was right next door.

We didn't have much time before sunrise. Once the latest night storm subsided, we'd fly to the shelter, keeping close to the ground. It would only take a few minutes and under the cover of dark, there was a chance we could avoid detection by the Consulate ship.

Everyone left the room to grab the containers of Caelia

Pure to transfer to the shelter for now. Kale also packed up the vitamin supplements, energy packets, and other key cargo in case the ship got raided. Everyone except James, who riffled through the various cabinets in the med room and gathered first-aid supplies and medications. He fingered one small box of pain tablets and turned to me. "Did you want anything for pain? I didn't want to give you any medication without your permission."

Right. He certainly didn't have a problem getting me naked without my permission. I opened my mouth to refuse, but my own small stash of painkillers flashed in my mind. Plan B. It would be stupid to turn down something that could be useful later.

"No, I don't want any now. You should bring them though. You know, just in case."

His brow wrinkled, but he slipped the box into the supply bag. He surveyed the room and turned to me. I tried to forget I was still naked save for a bit of white fabric. "I'm going to take this stuff up front. Your clothes are on the table over there . . . you should get dressed."

He's seen you without a stitch of those clothes on. I snorted. "You mean you're not going to stick around like last time I was naked."

James sighed. "I told you, I did what was necessary to help you." He waved his hand over the door panel and it slid open.

I called after him. "So, you were only focused on my injury. You didn't notice anything else."

James turned around, a serious look still on his face but a spark in his eyes. "I didn't say that." He went through the door before I could respond. It closed behind him.

My mouth hung open in the empty room. I should be angry with him, yet a small part of me liked the look on his face. Then reality kicked in. Here I was, injured and surrounded by enemies, yet worried about a medic seeing my body. Had my father taught me nothing?

I lowered myself down to the floor, and dressed as quickly as I could, wincing as I raised my arms to pull on my faded gray T-shirt. My gun lay next to my clothes. After dressing, I powered up the gun and moved to the door while trying to ignore the lingering nausea. I waved my hand over the door panel, and it opened easily.

The hallway lights buzzed faintly above me as I moved through the hall. The walls were a faded gray, like the color of a dead person. The only decorations were an assortment of dents and chips. This ship looked older than dirt. How it could fly fifty yards, let alone across the galaxy, was beyond me. How did they get here from Caelia on this piece of crap?

I passed a room to my right containing four sleep chambers. Clothes were strewn over two of the sleep pads, while another was neatly made with clothes folded atop it. Clothes that looked like Kale's military ones. The other chamber didn't appear like it had ever been slept in. Why was Kale sleeping with the crew? More important, why was he working against his own government, and how did James and Britta get involved in all this?

Another door stood open farther down the hall. I knew I shouldn't snoop, but curiosity got the best of me. Darkness saturated the room. I reached my hand inside, waving around for the light panel. The space lit up and I stepped inside. This had to be the captain's quarters. It contained just one enormous sleep chamber. I closed the door behind me so I wouldn't be seen from the hallway. The orderliness of the room impressed me. Not a thing out of place. Nothing to even suggest anyone lived there, aside from a pair of shoes lined up neatly by the door. A small clothing container rested against the wall. I couldn't resist.

I quickly opened the top drawer. Socks. Lots of socks. All white. Folded in matching pairs, as if it mattered, because they were all white. What did I think I'd find in here? I started to close it when I noticed something in contrast to the white, underneath one of the sock pairs in the far corner of the drawer. I moved the socks aside and pulled out a picture. No one printed out pictures anymore; they were too fragile. Viewing photos on an e-reader gave you living, breathing, three-dimensional images versus the flatness of the thermoplastic paper I held in my hand.

A cute little blond boy with hazel eyes stared up at me. I knew instantly it was James. He must have been five or six years old, and his smile radiated out from the photo. Surrounding him were a man and woman I assumed were his parents, and a smaller blond girl with eyes identical to his. They stood close together, the mother's hands around each of the children's shoulders. They looked happy. My eyes pulled back to James and that smile. It was a real smile. I couldn't imagine anyone who had to endure the harsh existence of Earth being happy, yet my sister had been that way too. Maybe someone who loved you enough to shield you from reality could keep the sadness away.

Except if the person who made James happy died, maybe the weight of the world crushed him in the aftermath. The few smiles I'd seen from him didn't reach his eyes the way this one did. The mere fact that he brought the picture everywhere meant that he'd loved his family a lot—maybe even loved his sister as much as I loved mine. I pushed the picture back under the socks and shut the drawer. Why were James' things in the captain's quarters? Maybe James needed his space here too? I needed some answers, and fast.

I opened another drawer filled with perfectly folded T-shirts. He really had an aversion to color because there was nothing but white here either. I lifted one to my nose and inhaled. It was clean, yet still smelled faintly like James, and somehow a little like the ocean. *Get a grip, it's a stupid shirt.* Impulsively, I took the folded shirt and tucked it under the waistband of my drawstring pants. The loose fit of my pants might not win any fashion awards, but they proved to be quite functional. I pulled my T-shirt down over my pants, covering the shirt.

I'd never stolen a thing in my life, yet a guy's shirt was shoved into my pants. I couldn't explain the sudden compulsion to take something of his, and I definitely wouldn't be able to justify it to the others if I got caught. *Maybe you do have oxygen deprivation.* I had to get out of there. They would wonder where I was by now.

This time the hallway beyond the doorway was darkened. Maybe they were the kind of high-tech lights my dad had installed in the shelter that would only light up when they sensed human energy. I stepped into the hallway. Nope. It stayed dark. I felt around for a light panel on the wall. After locating one, I waved my hand over it.

Light flooded the space. "There, that's better—"

Something connected with the back of my already bruised head and I went down hard on my face. Trigger flew from my hand and skittered across the floor. A humming echoed in my ear at the same time the hard sole of a boot pressed down into my back. I knew that hum. It was one of their guns. My ribs felt like they cracked in a few new places, and excruciating pain shot up my spine. A high-pitched chuckle came from above me. *Stupid bitch.*

"I can't wait to turn your ass over to them," Britta said.

Great. I could guess which "them" she was talking about. Britta and the others would probably run off with the guns as soon as they threw me at the Consulate. They'd have the guns, the Consulate would have me, and all I'd have was a lousy T-shirt.

Chapter TEN

BRITTA YANKED MY HANDS BACK FARTHER AND FORCED PLAStic electronic cuffs around my wrists. The motion made my entire rib cage feel like it was cracking apart. I'd made a huge mistake refusing those pain meds. She pushed her finger on a small button on the cuffs, and they shrank to the size of my wrists, ensuring there was no way I'd escape them.

She pulled me to my feet with one arm, demonstrating surprising strength for her petite birdlike frame. I'd read once that birds were descendants of a horrible creature called *Tyrannosaurus rex*. If nothing else, I finally understood the evolutionary process. The gun pointed straight at my left temple. "Scream and I'll muzzle you. Got it?"

She shoved me toward a small hallway. I guessed she

was not taking me to the main hatch where everyone was going to rendezvous. As soon as the ship touched down, we were supposed to race from the hatch to the shelter.

It wouldn't take more than a few minutes before someone would come looking to see what the holdup was. What the hell did she think she'd do with me? I'd be useless to the Consulate dead—I couldn't operate the stupid guns. As much as Britta disliked me, I'd only be helpful to her if I was alive and kicking.

"I'm guessing you're not following Kale's plan," I remarked.

Britta spoke in a low voice. "I'm following my own plan. I have to look out for myself."

That sounded like something I'd say. Before I had time to ponder this, she nudged me in the back toward a room at the end of the hall. Britta waved her hand over the door panel. When it opened, she pushed me inside and followed me into the space.

"Totally unnecessary push," I said and struggled to retain my balance. The cuffs dug into my wrists as I tried to yank my hands free.

I peered around the room. It looked like a storage area with strange containers inside. Britta waved her hand over a light panel, and a small hatch door illuminated on the far side of the room. Sweat broke out above my lip. No one was around and she really hated me. Was she planning to push me out the service entrance and let me cook in the sun? Oh, God, I really didn't want to die the way my sister did. Britta walked over to the odd containers and pushed a button. One container lit up and made a buzzing noise. Then the entire top of the rectangular-shaped box popped open.

Britta pointed at the box. "Get in."

I'd never been a claustrophobic kind of gal—after all, I lived in an underground cave half of my life. However, this little box looked like it could only contain, well, me.

"Look, I'm sure we can work something else out." I tried to twist and turn my hands in an attempt to escape the handcuffs, but they were so tight, I'd started to lose feeling in my fingers.

Britta came toward me. "Don't bother. You'll just hurt yourself." I struggled against her grip, though each movement caused fresh pain to tear through my ribs. "Don't worry." She steered me to the box. "It's a human transport container."

Britta pointed at the hatch door. "These containers are for emergency evacuations in space. You have several days' worth of air in there and the container emits an emergency signal—like a beacon. Since we're already on the ground, you'll just be right outside there." She gestured toward the hatch. A thoughtful look crossed her face before she shrugged. "I think these things hold up in the storms. I've never tested it out myself."

She shoved me hard again, and forced me to step into the box. "Don't take this personally. I mean, you're not my favorite person in the world, but it's not like I'm killing you or anything. You're just helping me out."

"Remind me how this helps you again."

Britta rolled her eyes. "Duh. My goal is to survive. When the Consulate gets my message about where to find you—their precious gun operator—they'll rescue you, which will distract them. Meanwhile, we'll be in the shelter, finding the guns. Then we'll take them and run for it. Even if they saw our ship, they wouldn't shoot us down with the weapons on it, or they'd lose everything. Kale can escape them."

She put her hand on my shoulder, pressing hard to make me sit. "The others won't be upset with me, because I'm going to tell them that right before we took off, you ran away to turn yourself in to the Consulate."

I had to stall for more time. Even if she didn't shoot me, being stuck in a small box seemed like it wouldn't turn out so well. I shook my head, trying to sound cocky. "So, is this where I point out the flaws in your grand plan because one, the others know I wouldn't go out into the night storms on my own, and two, do you really think the Consulate won't find you?"

"They'll believe what I tell them. Besides, with you out of the way, maybe we can get out of here a little faster. Now lie down. I only have a few minutes." She pointed the gun at me and pushed me down, which wasn't difficult since I couldn't offer much resistance.

I flopped down, sucking in my breath as my ribs stretched with the movement. The metal of the box grated against my skin. At least I wasn't going to be floating around space in this contraption. I wiggled my hands underneath me but they could barely move under the weight of my body. The box was so small that the sides pressed against my shoulders. *Good thing you're skinny and packed light.*

Britta pressed the button near my head. "I'd say I'll miss you, but I'd be lying."

I would have said something back, if the door hadn't clamped shut over my head, inches from my face. Sweat beaded on my lip. Despite the oxygen supply, I couldn't catch my breath. My rib situation wasn't helping matters either. I hoped the Consulate would find me quickly, because I didn't want to experience what several days in this box felt like.

A tiny window was positioned in the center of the box, above my face. I saw Britta move out of view in the direction of the hatch door. I realized the box must be soundproof because I heard nothing in my silent prison save for my own shallow breathing. I stared at the lights on the ceiling and hoped the window was sunproof, or I'd soon be staring straight at it. Getting rescued by the Consulate was looking better and better.

I closed my eyes and tried to calm myself by taking deep breaths. Inhale 1-2-3-4. Exhale 1-2-3-4. I tried to find my happy place, but that place involved my sister—and her charred body often surfaced in the midst of the memories and chased the good ones away. I squeezed my eyes tighter and attempted to relax.

A vision of my sister appeared. I saw the back of her

flowered shirt and her light golden hair flying behind her as I chased her down the hallway. No gray T-shirts for her. My dad paid a truckload for it too, but it was so worth it to see her smile. Her love of flowers extended to her wardrobe, as if by wearing them they weren't truly gone from the world. Her innocent laughter rang out as she raced to the table in the front room, which counted as "base" in our game. If she got there before I tagged her, she was safe. I ran harder, my hand reaching out to grasp the pink rosebud shirt. My fingers stretched and came close, yet touched only empty space.

The popping sound from above startled me. Had I already been evacuated into the desert and discovered by the Consulate? My eyes flew open. No, the lid of my container had been opened, and I was still in the same storage room. I sat up and looked straight ahead toward the hatch door. Britta was slumped on the ground in front of it.

"Are you okay?" James' deep voice tickled my ear.

I startled, a strangled cry escaping my throat.

"Sorry, didn't mean to scare you. Just trying to save you," he said, grasping my arm to guide me to my feet. I swayed a little, and he gripped me more firmly. I turned to thank him but my voice failed me. We stared at each other longer than necessary. My pulse started racing as fast as it had a few minutes ago when I thought I was going to die. Great. Two things I could count on for tachycardia: fear of death and James.

"Thanks, I'm okay," I finally managed. I didn't realize

how heavily I was leaning on him until my foot caught on the edge of the container, and I started to tumble, helpless due to the handcuffs.

His arms wrapped around me and he caught me to him before I could fall. He was impossibly strong. Our faces were an inch apart and my body pressed against him. My heart felt like it was beating out of my chest, and I was certain he could feel it through his shirt. Was it me or did his breathing seem faster too? His hand moved around to the small of my back and a shiver went up my spine. But then he pressed gently on my arm to push me back to a standing position. Touching my back had only been to get leverage.

"Guess I should have taken these off first," he said. "Gotta find the electronic key." He pushed a few buttons on his com device and the cuffs expanded and fell to the floor. He sounded embarrassed.

"It's okay," I said, struggling to sound normal. An awkward silence filled the room. I rubbed at the raw skin on my wrists, trying to think of something to say. "So, about Britta. Is she . . . "

"No." He showed me the setting on his gun. "I tranquilized her. I wondered what was taking so long. Knowing Britta, I thought maybe she'd done something stupid. Which she did."

James tucked the gun into his waistband and removed a slim tele-com device from his pocket. He called Kale in the cockpit to inform him what had happened.

I cringed as I stepped toward the door, a sharp stabbing

pain running through my ribs. James put an arm around my shoulder. *He's only touching you because you're hurt—it means nothing.*

"Maybe a pain tab wouldn't be a bad idea," he said softly.

The idea was beyond tempting. Just a little something to ease the discomfort. Plus, if the med was all it was cracked up to be, it would do more than dull my physical symptoms; maybe it would take the edge off the wrenching pain I'd felt a moment ago when I'd opened my eyes to find my sister was gone—again. But that pain was all I had. It was the only emotion I was really comfortable with, aside from anger. After the numbness that set in for a year after she died, the pain was a welcome change. It helped me realize I was still alive. "No, thanks. I'll be fine."

James sighed beside me. "Everyone needs help once in a while."

I gestured at my rib cage. "I believe I did let you help me with this."

"Only because you were unconscious."

I smiled.

"We better get to the main hatch." He jerked his head in Britta's direction as he helped me into the hallway. "Kale can figure out what to do with her."

"She's a piece of work. I can't believe you and her—" I clamped my mouth shut.

"Can't believe we what?" He faced me and looked genuinely confused.

I gulped. "I thought that you two . . . you know, used to . . . go out or something."

Shock crossed his face. "Hell, no. What gave you that idea?"

Blood rushed to my cheeks. "I heard her say that you needed your space and I assumed . . . " I stopped, realizing how lame I sounded.

I felt his eyes on me as we walked toward the front of the ship. He had to notice the scorching blush across my face, and his silence made it worse. After another small eternity, he said, "I like my space . . . from everyone. It's not specific to Britta, although space from her is a bonus." Before I could ask anything, he rushed on, "You had a sister too, right? Markus told me."

I remembered the photograph from the drawer. Where was he going with this? I played dumb. "Yeah, I did. You mean you have a sister too?"

"Had." He looked straight ahead while he talked. "Then you would understand how losing people can change you."

I wanted to ask more but we reached the main door and found Markus waiting for us.

"Where's Britta?" Markus asked.

James and I exchanged glances. James explained about Britta as the ship rumbled beneath us and lifted into the air. Looking out the window, I watched as we rose over the ridge, almost skimming the ground. The boulders near the shelter door were visible, and thankfully, the Consulate ship was nowhere in sight.

Another minute and we touched down. The winds remained still and the first cracks of sunlight punched through the darkness. Dark red streaks of light permeated the sky, relentless in their assault on the night. The bright orb blazed open like the eye of an angry demon. It would overtake the night, day by day, piece by piece, until there was no more dark. Someday soon it would be everlasting daylight, all day, every day. Blazing light with no reprieve, until it swallowed the Earth and burned out completely. Only then would it be eternal night.

The ship landed less than twenty feet from the shelter door. We moved quickly in the cold. I carried the lightest bag due to my injury. I pressed my thumb to the door lock and it clicked open. Kale and Markus carried a bound and still-unconscious Britta to the shelter, then ran back to the ship for a few more supplies. I would have been fine with leaving her for the Consulate, but Kale thought they'd kill her. It figures they'd decide now was the time to get all ethical.

I stood watch atop the ladder. As James returned with his final load, Markus and Kale ran toward me with their bags. Their heads jerked up to the sky in unison. I turned around to see the giant Consulate ship rising from the east. It was heading right for us.

"Run!" I screamed. I pulled my gun from my waistband. I had to close the door or they'd kill us all. The ship's guns began firing as Markus reached the door. I moved to the side as he jumped straight down to the floor of the shelter.

Kale followed close behind but the ship bore down fast. The laser pulses came closer to me and I screamed for Kale to jump. He did.

The ship fired and hit the large boulder by the door, which sent shards of rock flying. A piece of it hit Kale as he fell through the hatch door. I shot at the ship and grazed one of its wings. A small plume of smoke billowed out, yet it remained airborne.

"Hannibal!" Kale screamed as he fell down the entry-way, landing with a hard thud at the bottom of the ladder. After firing one last shot at the ship, I scrambled inside and pulled the door closed behind me. The groan of the lock sliding into place echoed through the shelter.

James was already at Kale's side by the time I reached the bottom rung. Markus hobbled over, having sprained an ankle in his own jump. "How bad is he?" I asked James.

"He's just fine, thanks," Kale responded. His leg bled profusely from a large gash on the back of his calf.

"At least we have the supplies with us," said James. "Tora, can you hand me that bag?"

I tossed him the bag, glad that I wasn't the one whose leg looked like it had been turned inside out. At least there wasn't as much blood with my injury. I didn't do so well with blood. James worked quickly to stem the flow. To my eyes, it looked less like a laser wound and more like his leg had been gutted. Kale didn't refuse the pain meds like I had, but my wound hadn't looked like his. James pulled a small, shiny disk from the bag. When he turned it on, a triangle of red light emanated from it.

Markus leaned closer to get a better look but James put his arm up to stop him. "I wouldn't get too close to this if I were you." He aimed the red light at the back of Kale's leg, moving it slowly up and down the sliced open area. Even with the painkillers, Kale grunted in agony. The device was piecing his leg back together.

I gasped. I'd never seen anything like this before. Then again, my father specialized in weaponry, not medicine. "Wow," I said. "It's like energetic stitches."

"You'd think it'd be less painful than the regular kind," Kale said through gritted teeth.

James looked apologetic. "No, but the beam also sterilizes the area. Stops infection, which is the worst that could happen in a case like this. This way, you won't lose the leg."

Kale's eyes widened. He clearly hadn't considered that prospect. James worked so methodically and calmly that I realized how lucky we were to have a medic like him around. I only hoped we wouldn't need him again anytime soon. As great as the laser stitching contraption might be, I had no desire to have it focused on any of my body parts.

James finished bandaging Kale's leg. "You need to stay off it as much as possible. Try to get some rest for a few hours. Markus, I'll check out your ankle in a sec."

"Thanks, I'm thinking I owe you my life," said Kale.

"Then I guess we're even."

James owed Kale his life. I so needed to find out the details of that story. Markus and James helped Kale to his feet. Kale put an arm around each of their shoulders, and they started to move him to the couch. That was when the bomb hit.

Either the Consulate ship was no longer afraid I'd use the weapons or they thought breaking out their own bombs first would blow the shelter door off pretty quickly. A sonic boom rattled the entire shelter. Britta moaned, as if she was fighting her way back to consciousness—in her typical whiny fashion. A cup fell off the table, skittering across the floor. The W.A.R. machine moved several inches from its station but remained intact. Markus stumbled, almost bringing down Kale and James with him. He braced his hand against the wall to steady himself, a slew of curse words streaming from his mouth.

I grabbed onto the chair in front of me for support. The vibrations of the bomb continued to resonate through my weak ribs. I looked skyward at the hatch door. This was some serious stuff they were dropping on us. If that door didn't hold, I wouldn't have to worry about fending off Kale and keeping him away from the guns. I'd be too dead to care.

Chapter ELEVEN

A HALF AN HOUR WENT BY WITHOUT ANY NEW BLASTS. KALE had fallen into a heavy sleep thanks to the meds and we'd moved him to my sister's sleep chamber. I'd tucked James' shirt into my satchel where it wouldn't be discovered. Markus suggested everyone try to get a little shut-eye, and despite the fear of bombs overhead, I'd barely made it to my sleep pad before drifting off. I didn't know when I'd get the chance to rest again, so I had to make this nap count.

● ● ●

Markus, James, and I sat in the study, while Britta's whining could be heard all the way from the front room. She was demanding to be released from her restraints. I sat as far from Markus on the bench as I could, while James sat across from us.

"Can't we tranquilize her again? Maybe use some duct tape?" I begged James. He chuckled, which meant he thought I was kidding.

"How's the ankle holding up?" James asked Markus. He'd wrapped it and said the sprain seemed minor.

"It's holding I guess—just hurts like hell. I gotta say I'm a little worried though." Markus pointed upward where the Consulate was likely preparing a new attack. "We're all injured to some degree, except for you." He nodded at James. "It's only a matter of time before they get down here."

All I knew for sure about the door was that my father had it made special for the shelter. It looked and felt like some sort of super-metal, but I'd been so young at the time. I only recalled him telling me it would keep us safe. Though it had proven to be quite bomb-resistant, Markus was right. No matter how strong the door might be, it couldn't hold up forever. If the Consulate managed to either successfully bomb or otherwise compromise the door, they'd get down here. If they got down here, we'd all be toast. Unless . . .

Markus seemed to read my thoughts. "Look, I know your feelings about the weapons. You're the only one that can use them, so maybe it would be a good idea to get a bigger gun to use against those burners."

Several of the guns in containment could take out any Consulate jerk who tried to get down here. Others could take down their whole burner ship. One in particular would take out pretty much everything. The problem?

As soon as I opened up my secret room, it would lose the secret part. Nothing would stop Markus or Kale from taking the whole arsenal. I didn't know what good it would do them, but maybe they'd guessed it was possible for the Consulate to reprogram the guns. Hell, I worried about that myself. So maybe Kale thought they could still bargain with them. The power of the bombs coming down told me the Consulate was done bargaining.

"I don't know, Markus. Not that I don't trust you and all, but, well, I don't."

Britta's screeching started again, a high-pitched whine about her discomfort. I smiled sweetly at Markus, "Can you go deal with her, please?"

Markus stood. "Fine." He looked at James on the way out. "Can you please talk some sense into her while I'm gone?"

I steeled myself for the lecture about why I should bring out the big guns, so to speak. James watched me, not saying anything. He was no Markus, I'd give him that. I didn't want to talk about the guns anyway. I wanted to talk more about his sister and ask about the picture. Since I couldn't ask him that, I wasn't going to say anything. If he wanted silence, fine. I was done being the conversation starter.

My silence lasted two whole minutes. I totally broke first. "Why aren't you trying to convince me to get the guns?"

James glanced toward the hallway, like he didn't want

to be overheard. "Because I'm not sure that you should. I don't think you can trust them."

Them? "You say that as if you're not with them, as if you weren't shooting at me twenty-four hours ago."

"I didn't."

The air went out of my lungs. "What?" I whispered.

He stared down at the ground. "Markus showed us a picture of you back on Caelia, it was on his com device, and—"

"Hold up. Markus has a picture of me? From when?"

James' eyes briefly met mine before looking away again. "I don't know. You looked so sad and . . . anyway, when you came out of this shelter, even though you had the suit on, I kept seeing the girl in the picture. I couldn't shoot."

It took a minute before I remembered Markus' visit right before he left to find Caelia. Markus had pulled his tele-com out of his pocket and aimed it at me. "Smile, Tora, so I have something to remember you by if I don't make it back." I hadn't smiled. "You better make it back. You're my Plan A for getting outta here," I'd told him. I hadn't mentioned Plan B.

Had he known then what he was going to do? Was he already planning to steal the guns?

"I don't know, James. It sure seemed like gunfire was coming from every suit out there." I wanted to believe him but how naive would that make me?

"Oh, I shot all right. The ground, the rocks near you, but not you. I'm a pretty good shot. I knew the others weren't aiming to kill anyway, so I figured I didn't need to help."

Arrogant much? "So you're saying if you had tried to shoot me, you could have."

He replied with a shrug. Infuriating, yes. But if what James was saying was true, he'd never tried to hurt me. *Yeah, but he let other people try to hurt you.*

His eyes gleamed as he studied me. "Of course, if Markus had said what a pain in the ass you could be, I might've aimed differently."

I smirked at him. "You're pretty funny when you want to be."

He smiled but his words were heavy. "Thanks. Not much opportunity for funny lately."

"Where's your family?" The words flew out of my mouth before I could grab them back. I gulped. "I mean, you mentioned having a sister too."

"I don't really like to talk about it." His eyes hardened.

I ignored the surge of sympathy that welled up. I needed answers, not the silent treatment. "Okay, so then let's talk about why your things are in the captain's quarters, shall we?"

James leaned forward, his elbows on his knees, hands clasped in front of him. Against my better judgment, my heart pounded at the close proximity of our bodies. "You ask a lot of questions, you know that?" His eyes drilled into mine. "Okay, I'll tell you, but then I have a question for you." He looked down at his hands. "So my sister—"

"Spartacus! Why does my leg feel like someone set it on fire and then pissed on it?"

James smiled at me. "Guess somebody's pain meds wore off."

"What's up with all the names?" I asked.

James laughed. "Oh, that. Kale is one of the hardest core military guys you'll ever meet. He's obsessed with ancient military heroes."

I shook my head. "He uses military names as curse words?"

James nodded and stretched as he walked toward the door. His shirt lifted—a strange jagged scar ran across his lower back. It looked too precise to be an injury. His body couldn't keep secrets the way his mouth could. Another question for my list if I could get him alone again. He turned around at the door and caught me staring at his back. James tugged his shirt down. He whispered, "Seriously, Tora. Don't trust them."

What the hell was I supposed to do with that information? I already knew I couldn't trust the Consulate, Kale, or Britta. Dad had told me long ago not to trust anyone if anything happened to him. Yet he had trusted Markus, who turned out to be a burner, so putting my trust in James would make me just as dumb. I couldn't let him get to me no matter how amazing his abs were. Still, that sadness in his eyes—

Another bomb rocked the bunker, and I almost fell out of my seat. I gasped as the lamp in the study crashed to the floor. My father got it at an antique trade market years ago. Lamps hadn't been used in ages. The one benefit of Earth's demise was that we got a truckload of solar energy. Special solar cell panels provided all the light any one person could use. We only had two panels, disguised as part of the cactus grove, and we could light this place up like a Christmas cactus if we wanted.

"Everyone doin' okay?" Markus asked.

I reached the front room and noticed Britta sitting near Markus. Scratch the near part; she was almost in his lap. His hand rested lightly on her cuffed ones. Guess he wasn't too disturbed by her trying to send me on a one-way ticket out of here.

Kale hobbled in, refusing James' offers of assistance. "I'm not sure it's a good idea for you to be bearing weight on it yet—"

"Nonsense. Am I the damn captain of this team or what? I walk when I want to walk. Nobody tells me when the hell to walk." He grimaced as he hopped to the nearest chair and parked himself in it.

Markus looked over at James. "Is he drunk or something?"

"Nah, just the pain meds can have a similar effect. He'll probably fall asleep again soon."

"Dammit! I don't want any more sleep. I want to get the hell out of here."

I thought of their ship. It was unlikely that it was even

in one piece, so I didn't think we were going anywhere. I told him so.

Kale laughed long and hard. Yeah, he sounded drunk. "They didn't drop the bombs on the ship, I guaran-fucking-tee it. Tora hit their wing so they'll save our ship in case they need it. But they won't get far." He started laughing again, then reached in his pocket and pulled out a small metallic object. It looked like a machine part.

Britta's eyes widened. She was probably wondering if her fearless leader had totally lost his mind. She looked ridiculous, but I had to admit, I wondered the same thing myself.

"What is that, Kale?" asked James in the gentle tone one uses to talk to a child. His gravelly voice soothed me and I wasn't even the one freaking out.

"Just a little thing my ship can't fly without—the fuel converter. Those burners aren't goin' anywhere in our ship." He chuckled a minute, then dropped his head on the table and started snoring.

Markus laughed. "Wow. Nice meds there, James." He cleared his throat, and pulled his hand back from Britta's. "So, in light of what's going on here, don't you think we should take off Britta's cuffs? She's promised to be a good girl."

Britta scowled at me. Nothing about her looked remotely good. I fought to keep my temper, but it never allowed itself to be kept for long. "Markus, I realize this pint-sized burner raises the flag on your flagpole so to speak, but no way in hell is she getting out of those. She'd just attack me again."

"I didn't attack you." She spat the words at me. "Well, okay, I did, but it wasn't like I tried to kill you or anything."

Right. Because leaving me in a locked coffin for the Consulate was a total act of kindness.

"Please, these cuffs are killing me." Her tone changed to that of a petulant child.

I couldn't help laughing. "Yeah, like I wouldn't know how that feels, right?"

"Fine, I'm . . . I'm . . . sorry." Britta almost choked on the last word. It had to be the first apology she'd given in her life. She did look miserable though.

I looked to James, but he deferred to me. "It's your call." He stared at Britta. "But Britta, I'll take you down myself if you try to sabotage the plan again. You didn't follow orders and that's punishable by death. You of all people should know that."

A long look passed between them, one I didn't understand.

"Fine," Britta said. "But he doesn't seem capable of giving orders right now, so that makes you in charge."

"Only until he wakes up, which should be in less than an hour. What do you say, Tora?"

James' deference surprised me. He was certainly trying to make the case that I could trust him. It was a shame I didn't have an ounce of trust to spare. I wondered if the "punishable by death" thing would apply if I told Kale about James not shooting at me earlier. If so, he trusted me more than I would have if I were him.

"You can release her." A small surge of pleasure ran through me at having power over Britta. A taste of her own medicine.

James pushed the electronic release button, and Markus removed her cuffs. Britta rubbed her wrists vigorously, like she'd been confined for weeks in a dark dungeon, instead of an hour on the couch.

We sipped water, trying to be civil to one another while rotating door patrol and bracing as each round of bombs dropped. Kale finally woke up, swearing up one side and down the other.

"Sorry, sir, no more pain meds. We need you."

"Zulu! What's a man gotta do to get good medical help these days?" Kale bitched and moaned but James refused to give him any more meds. Markus handed Kale a water bottle instead, which Kale promptly threw against the wall. Thank God the lid was still on it; wasting water was unheard of. I'd never seen a man have a temper tantrum before, but he finally calmed down after realizing he wasn't getting any more painkillers.

Kale took a long chug from the water bottle Britta had retrieved from the floor. "So, did you figure out a game plan in my absence?" he asked.

Looks passed back and forth among everyone. No one wanted to be the one to say there was no game plan.

James addressed him. "Sir—"

"Yes, we have a plan," I interrupted. All heads swiveled to me. James had a questioning look in his eyes, like he was still trying to warn me. I might not be able to trust the rest of them and I might later regret my decision, but part of me must have decided to trust him. The words rushed out before I could stop them. "I'm getting the guns."

Chapter TWELVE

I LED JAMES DOWN THE CORRIDOR TOWARD THE RECREATION room, then beyond it to the closet. I'd forced everyone else into the front room. James and I would bring the guns up to them. I didn't want anyone else back there with us because a) I didn't trust them even more than I didn't trust James and b) I hadn't yet decided whether I was bringing all of the guns or not. I was thinking of the most deadly ones. If I left the really bad ones there, maybe James wouldn't tell.

Scratch that. It wouldn't work to leave some in the room. The Consulate knew Dad had completed all the weapons—Dad told me he'd shown them T.O. right before he took off. They'd come looking for it faster than you could say *pistola*. I'd have to take them with me, and figure out what to do with them later.

As we reached the closet, I took out a stack of towels and placed them on the floor, then waved my hand over a hidden panel in the back of the door. It had been programmed to only accept my father's hand and mine.

"I knew it," said James, as the back of the closet swung inward, taking the rest of the linen-filled shelves with it.

"Of course you did." I rolled my eyes at him.

He had the decency to look embarrassed. "I didn't know for sure. It's just when I came to find a towel for my workout yesterday, it seemed like the logical place for a secret room to be." He waved his arm ahead of him like a gentleman. "After you."

"Is there anything you don't know?" I huffed and stepped through the small entryway. Pitch blackness enveloped us.

I heard him step through the doorway behind me and I turned to find the light panel. He leaned so close I could feel his breath on my face in the darkness. He spoke in a low voice. "There's plenty I don't know."

My heart pounded in my chest. The effect he had on my body was so unfair. It was probably exactly what he wanted too. That would make it easier for all of them to screw me over. I wouldn't let it happen.

I took a step away from him. "You mean like where the light panel is?" I felt along the wall and located it. The lights clicked on, flickered a little, then held a steady glow. James stared at me, like he wanted to say something, then turned and surveyed his surroundings like a good soldier.

Several boxes were stacked in a back corner of the rectangular-shaped room, some empty and others filled with the garden variety guns like Kale and his crew had. Dad thought it was a good idea to keep some around "just in case." He was big on "just in case" things.

Clear cases lined the four walls of the room and each one contained different weapons. Every case had its own panel lock on it. I'd be doing a lot of hand waving. Good thing it was my ribs and not my wrist that was injured.

James let out a low whistle. "These are some serious guns."

"That's why my dad got paid the big bucks. Until he stole them, anyway." I followed James' eyes to the center of the large room. He hadn't noticed it at first. I didn't blame him. There was an island there about waist high and three feet long. It was completely clear, so it was almost invisible if you weren't looking right at it. It appeared to hold nothing. I knew better.

I pretended I didn't see the question in his eyes and started at the first panel. "I'll get this group out and we'll take them up first. We should be able to get them all in two trips." I gestured at the boxes in the corner. "We can pack them in those. Except for the one I'll use on the Consulate ship." Without waiting for a response, I waved my hand over the first lock and began removing the guns, being careful not to power them up as I touched them.

James' voice washed over me. "What happened to your dad? Markus said he . . . died."

The desire to open up to him was strong. My resolve to get answers was stronger. "I believe you still owe me the rest of your story first . . . about your sister."

"Oh, yeah, that story." He sighed and looked straight ahead at the wall. "It started when I stole the W.A.R. machine . . . after my family's machine had started to break down, along with our air unit. I'd already sealed off the other rooms in the pod to maximize the oxygen saturation, so we all slept in the center room."

His voice was steely. "I knew a W.A.R. violation could result in death but I thought my gun would be enough to protect my mom, dad, and little sister." James turned from the imaginary spot on the wall and faced me. "They came in the middle of the night, despite the night storms, so I was caught off guard. My gun was across the room when they came in. The officers saw it and seized it, assuming it was Dad's. My little sister clung to me, screaming, when they shot him. He died instantly." He described how his mother's cries ended in the sharp sounds of more gun blasts.

James' jaw muscle twitched, the only giveaway that this story caused him pain. He clenched his fist and took a deep breath. "I begged them to spare my sister. Told them it was all my fault and she had nothing to do with it." He punched one of the gun cases. "They said that the world didn't need another worthless child to feed and they shot her, her arms still wrapped around me."

My heart strained, sadness pouring into the space inside me that I tried to keep empty. Tears leaked from my eyes, and I fought the urge to hug him the way my sister used to hug me. I thought of how he tried to protect everyone by keeping them in the same room. "So the space thing . . ."

His voice was hard. "People are safer if they aren't around me . . . or at least I'm not responsible if they die. I know it's not rational but that's how I feel. The only solo room on the ship was the captain's. Kale offered it to me without me asking." He looked back into my eyes. "Your turn."

I hadn't told anyone the full story, not even Markus. Yet it was only fair after everything James just told me. "Dad was told the guns were for the relocation program. In case the government ran into hostile species while exploring new planets. That was partially true, but he found out later they were also going to be used for another reason. He wouldn't say anything other than it would be 'against our own.'"

James gritted his teeth, like he had an idea what Dad was referring to. I paused, but he shook his head.

"Anyway, they tricked him into coming to a meeting in the pod city. They said they wanted to come to an agreement about the guns, that they understood his position. I think he wanted to believe it was true. That with so few people left in the world, there had to be some good in them. He was wrong." I pulled another gun from its case and slid it toward James, not looking at him. He stacked it in the crate.

"He never came back from that trip. The story was on

the GlobalNet several days later—one of the last before the entire broadcasting system collapsed. I thought it was because they all died. I didn't know they'd found a new planet. They showed a picture of my father's abandoned land cruiser and claimed he was found in the wastelands outside their sector. Liars. They murdered him and had the nerve to plead that any surviving relatives contact the Consulate for assistance." I swallowed.

It was ironic that my father worried the cruiser itself would give us away, as he'd flown it back and forth from the shelter to the pod city. He'd kept it hidden as much as possible behind the cactus grove, and the Consulate would have found it had they searched long enough. In a way, I was lucky they had found Caelia when they did.

My eyes filled with tears. I forced them back. I didn't have time for emotion. I pulled out two more guns and brought them to James. "Here, take these. One more case, and we'll bring this load up front. Then we'll do the next batch."

His hand touched mine a second longer than was necessary, as I handed him the guns. "I'm sorry about . . . your dad."

My eyes met his. "Thanks. I'm sorry about your family too."

He nodded and looked so close to saying something more. But he only shifted the guns in his arms.

We took the first load of about a hundred guns to the front and Kale's face lit up as soon as he laid eyes on them.

"So these are the legendary bioweapons. Mind if I hold one?"

I gritted my teeth. His excitement was nauseating. These guns were the reason my father was dead. How could you be excited over something when its only purpose was to destroy? "Go for it."

Kale pulled one off the top of the pile and stroked it like it was alive. He put his thumb over the power panel. Nothing happened. "You weren't kidding then. No one can use them except you?"

"Like I would've let you lay a finger on it if it would work for any of you."

Kale looked thoughtful. "You're not worried that someone would cut off your thumb so they'd have your print any time they wanted it?"

Something about the way Kale said it sent a shiver down my spine. I liked him better when he was high on pain meds. "It's not my thumbprint that powers it. It's my vibration." I stared at him coldly. "And in case you had any other bright ideas, you have to be living to vibrate, so cutting anything off won't help you."

Kale studied me. "Calm down. I wasn't thinking of cutting you, Tora. I'm just remarking on how smart your father was."

We might be in the same boat for now, but it was pretty clear that Kale jumped into any boat that wasn't sinking. And ours sprang new leaks with every impact of the incoming bombs.

I really needed to use the bathroom before going back to the weapons room. "Be right back," I said.

After using the recycling machine, I observed my dark hair in the mirror and sighed. Nothing would tame my wild locks. I tucked a wayward strand behind my ear and combed through the ends with my fingers, then froze. What the hell was I doing? My father had taught me better than to primp for a boy, especially one of the burner variety. I shook my hair back out and marched into the front room.

Markus had moved to the table. He and Kale were discussing something about ship engine mechanics. What bothered me was James. He sat next to Britta, whispering in her ear. She leaned into him, nodding. Their bodies were almost touching; it looked—intimate. They didn't even notice I'd returned. Had he lied about their being together? Nothing he did or said should bother me, so why did seeing them so close together make my stomach turn?

"Are you ready?" My voice came out harsher than expected, and James looked startled.

He stood quickly. "Yeah."

We walked in silence to the back room. I was so not doing any more talking.

"Everything okay?" he asked.

"Sure." That's all I would give him. Not another word.

He touched my arm as we ducked through the doorway again into the weapons room. Tingles ran through me, which pissed me off. I was onto his game. He wanted to get me to trust him so he could take me down.

His thumb lightly rubbed my forearm. "Tora?" My heart sped up and my knees went weak. "What's wrong?"

My body needed to stop reacting to him. I jerked my arm away. "What's up with all the whispering with bird girl?"

"Bird girl?" He had the nerve to look amused.

"Britta, the one you were all over just now. Were you plotting how to trick me?"

He shook his head. "I can't figure you out. I was just talking to her . . . about you." His fingers grazed my arm again as I tried to unlock another case. "Look, Kale is the one you need to worry about. Not me."

"Yeah, so you've said." I unlocked another gun case. "Remind me again why I should trust you but not Kale? You have to obey him, right?"

"Britta didn't when she knocked you out," said James. His brow furrowed. "But if she goes rogue again, Kale will show no mercy. It's funny. I owe him my life but I don't trust him with it."

I handed him an armful of guns and remained in front of him. "Sounds like there's a story there. Want to tell it?" I noticed he didn't seem to have any interest in holding the guns the way Kale did.

"It's a long story." His eyes held mine. "I promise I'll tell you everything soon . . . once I'm sure I can trust you completely." He said it in a teasing way, almost flirtatious, and my heart rate sped up again.

I arched an eyebrow. "That's funny. You're the one who doesn't seem very trustworthy. I'm an open book, I have nothing to hide." Though part of me wanted to trust him, trusting someone made you vulnerable. They could let you down. They could die. They could kill you.

He turned and faced the center of the room. "Nothing to hide, huh? So what's with the empty case here?"

I smiled despite myself. "Be patient. We have to finish these first." I clucked my tongue. "Just when I was thinking you didn't have an interest in these guns."

He smiled back and accepted another armload from me. "It's more curiosity than interest. I mean, look at us. Have guns made us better people? Better at killing things maybe, but I'm not sure that's much of a legacy."

My hand brushed his as I extricated myself from the weapons. I ignored the tingle of electricity that shot up my arm. "Ah, a philosopher-soldier. How interesting."

I opened the last case on the second wall and fingered one of the guns as I removed it. I remembered this one. This was one of the ones my father made me practice with for hours at a time. *Aim well, Tora, because whatever you hit won't exist afterward.* There had been many additional boulders near our shelter door in the past. I'd obliterated them during target practice, so I named the gun Boulder-Killer—B.K. for short, which was only slightly more creative than naming my first gun Trigger. I'd taken B.K. and planned to destroy the rock where I'd found my mother and sister dead, but changed my mind. I kept the rock to remember the pain.

James watched me handle the gun. "If you don't mind my saying, your father placed an awful lot of responsibility on you by making you the sole operator of these things."

A sigh escaped my lips. "He didn't key them to his own vibration, because I think he knew deep down that they'd kill him eventually. If I could use the guns, I could protect myself from the Consulate. It's why he trained me."

I told James how he'd made the guns as ordered in the beginning. "They were powered by human energy the same way Infinities and other devices were. When he realized the magnitude of destruction his creations could cause, he changed his mind. He keyed the gun panels to my specific energy vibration. Because the likelihood of two people having the same vibration is about nil, only slightly more probable than identical fingerprints, he figured it was a smart move. He chose me. My sister was younger than me and he didn't want to involve her. My mother . . . well, yeah. Anyway, I guess my father's plan was genius, since they died and all." I heard the harsh tone in my voice but couldn't help it.

"How did they die?"

I choked back a sob. I didn't know how they died. No, that wasn't true. I knew how they died. They cooked alive. The better question was why, but I had no answer for that. How could they die so close to our shelter door? Why were they outside without their suits on? Did they even try to get inside? No matter how many times I went over it in my head, I came up blank. My voice squeaked out. "I don't know what happened exactly. Why the hell am I telling you so much, anyway?"

I grabbed another case and dumped the guns inside, but I had a choice to make. I rubbed my fingers over Trigger—she'd been my constant companion over the years. A loyal and reliable weapon, and I'd never forget how she'd saved me from Markus several weeks ago. But I needed something with more power. "Good-bye for now, Trigger." I placed Trigger into the crate, ignoring James' stare, and tucked Boulder-Killer into my waistband.

I wiped my damp forehead with the back of my arm and went to the island in the center. "Just one more."

James walked over to my side. He tucked a sweaty lock of my hair behind my ear. "We've both lost people we loved, Tora."

I shivered at his touch and tried to remain calm. I turned and looked into his eyes. "Yeah, so?"

His eyes didn't let go of mine. "So maybe we *can* trust each other is all."

We stood just a foot apart from each other. The green flecks in his eyes seemed to shift, merging with the brown and then changing again. His eyes were almost as impressive as his abs. The silence grew and the ghost of a smile curved on his lips. The charged feelings running through my body were way beyond my comfort zone. I broke eye contact, my thudding heart reminding me that I wasn't in control. "We, um, really should finish up here," I mumbled.

James nodded. We faced the clear rectangular case, and

I tried to ignore the heat I felt coming from his body. He needed to stay a good five feet away at all times in order for me to concentrate.

He ran his hand over the case, staring down into the empty space within it. "Were you and Markus together?" he asked.

That was not the question I expected. I laughed. "Give me a little more credit than that."

"Okay, but weren't you the one asking me about dating Britta?"

"Good point." I waved my hand over the top of the compartment. When I reached a special spot on the lower left corner, a panel lock appeared.

"Whoa, cool," said James. "I'm guessing it's not empty."

"Hardly." When the case unlocked, a small square panel in the top center of it opened toward us. I reached in and as my hand approached the center of the case, the object glowed.

James gasped. "It's invisible."

"Yeah, unless I'm touching it." I grasped it firmly and pulled it out.

James' eyes were wide. I couldn't help feeling a small surge of satisfaction. He didn't seem surprised by much, but he sure looked it now. "What the hell is it? It doesn't look like a gun."

I reached up through the center of it and touched the trigger of the spherical object. "I'm sure my dad once told me its technical name but I don't remember, because I've always called it The Obliterator, aka T.O."

"That sounds worse than a gun. It looks more like a bomb."

Damn he was smart, which only made him cuter. I nodded. "A bomb that fires like a gun. If I powered up and pressed the trigger, everything within a twenty-mile radius of me would be wiped out."

James whistled. "Everything except you, right? Because it's keyed to your . . . "

"Vibration," I finished. "Right. Only something vibrating at my exact same speed would survive." I removed my hand from the weapon's center and rubbed the smooth, polished surface. "He designed it as a last-resort weapon. I don't even aim it, just press the button."

"Pretty cool," said James. "You could take down a whole fleet by yourself."

"Yeah, and all of you." I tried to say it like I was joking, but James didn't look amused.

I shifted The Obliterator to my other hand and pulled B.K. out of my waistband. "Don't worry. B.K. here will take care of that ship outside. I just need one good shot."

"You have nicknames for all your guns?"

"Of course—guns are the closest thing to pets I've had. I was ten when I had to learn how to use them so naming them made it more fun. Here, can you hold Boulder-Killer a sec while I figure out how to hide T.O. under my clothes?"

James slowly looked up and down my body, which

made my cheeks burn, yet he looked all business as he took the gun. "Absolutely."

"Oh, please. It's nothing you haven't seen before," I said, my face blushing hotter.

James' eyes burned as he looked at me, into me. I turned away and lifted my shirt. T.O. wasn't huge but it wasn't minuscule either—big enough to accommodate my finger in its center. Its shape was even more problematic. Ball-shaped items did not make for easy hiding. My drawstring pants and T-shirt were loose, but not loose enough. The weapon stuck out too much from my back pocket, making it look like I had a tumor on my ass. Plus, I didn't want to accidentally sit on something that lethal. I tried the front pocket, but it was too big to even fit inside.

"Everything okay?" he asked, giving an exaggerated yawn.

I called over my shoulder. "Sorry if I'm boring you but I'm having issues here."

James laughed. "I see that. I'd be happy to help."

I scowled at him, which only made him laugh louder. "Don't worry, I promise I won't look." His own gun was tucked in his waistband, and he waved B.K. around as he walked toward me. "Have no fear," he said, striking a mock pose with my gun and aiming at the wall, "Boulder-Killer is here." He put his finger on the trigger panel.

I don't know which one of us was more surprised when the gun went off.

Chapter THIRTEEN

THE LASER HIT THE FIRST CASE ON THE WALL, SHATTERING IT to bits.

"What the—?" James dropped the gun, as if it were on fire.

Footsteps pounded down the hallway outside, and I hesitated a second before shoving The Obliterator into my bra. I scrambled toward B.K. but didn't get there in time.

Kale burst into the room, gun drawn, swearing up and down about having to run down the hall on a bum leg. Markus and Britta followed him. At least they hadn't given her a gun too. She would have shot first and asked questions later. Kale looked from James to me, appearing confused that neither of us had a gun in hand. I stood about a foot from James, with B.K. on the ground between us.

"What in the holy hell is going on in here?" he asked.

"I accidentally fired the gun when I got it out of the case," I said, bending to pick it up while keeping a hand over my chest, so my lethal right boob didn't roll out onto the floor.

Kale looked around the room, frowning. His eyes rested on the center case right behind me, then fell on James. "Is that what happened?"

James still looked shaken. "Yes, sir. She scared the crap out of me."

"We better get moving," I said. Markus' eyes met mine with a steely gray stare. He didn't believe me. He couldn't have known what happened, but he sure didn't believe my version of the story. His gaze traveled down to my chest and my larger right breast. Only Markus would notice that, the perv.

I ignored him and pushed my way through the group and into the hallway. What did happen? There's no way James could have fired the gun, unless he was vibrating at the exact speed as me—an almost statistical impossibility.

Kale hadn't been able to activate the guns when he had tried, and I had no doubt that Markus and Britta had given it a shot while we were back here. Which means the fact that James fired it was no fluke. I stopped in my room and grabbed a brown satchel, then removed T.O. from my bra. I placed it into the smaller inner compartment of the bag. As soon as I zipped the pocket closed, the seam disappeared and became invisible. No one would know it was there. I slung it over my head, with the strap diagonal across my body so that my injured ribs were on the opposite side. The others might be suspicious that I'd taken to wearing a bag, but I couldn't help that. This weapon needed to stay safe.

"When's it gonna be night again? They'll have to go away when the storms start, right?" Britta moaned.

"Not for a few hours yet." Kale stretched. "Be patient."

Markus leaned down and picked something up off the floor. "We shouldn't be too patient. I'm only saying that because this fell from the door when the last bomb hit. It looks sort of important." He held up a screw.

The indestructible door was falling apart. Something close to panic set in. "Not good," I agreed.

The blast of another bomb almost knocked me off my feet, and Britta hung on to the chair as the room rattled. Kale cursed as the table knocked into his injured leg. As soon as the aftershocks settled, I'd make my move. It was the perfect time. I suited up, and turned on B.K.

"You don't have to do this by yourself." James' low voice sliced through the air. "Let me come with you."

I shook my head. "I'm the one with the cool weapon, remember? No use in the rest of you getting hurt."

Markus touched my arm in a halting way. "Be careful up there. Take your best shot and get back down here."

Kale nodded. "Aim for the underside of the ship in the back end. It's where the engine is."

"Great, because it would be pretty hard to hit the top of the ship from the ground."

"Always the smart-ass," said Markus.

James smiled at me until he noticed Britta staring at him. His somber expression returned quickly.

I raised my gun and started toward the ladder. "I want to time opening the door just right. I want to go out, aim, shoot, and get back inside."

The aftershocks lasted longer this time. They were getting weaker though. Maybe I could make it up the ladder before another bomb hit. As I reached the bottom rung, a heavy creaking noise sounded above me. Several pings echoed as small objects bounced off my helmet. More screws. Before I could react, an arm came from behind me, pulling me to the ground.

The heavy shelter door crashed to the floor, inches from my feet. Several additional screws and pebbles scattered across the room from the impact. James fell on top of me, shielding my body with his. Our faces were so close that the only thing separating us was the clear plate of my helmet.

"You okay?" he said loudly, like the helmet made me deaf or something.

"Yeah," I yelled back just as loud, eliciting another smile from him. "Thanks for saving my ass."

"I hate to break this little love fest up," said Markus. "But I have to point out the obvious. We. Have. No. Door. Maybe the perfect timing you were talking about could be like, now."

James scrambled off me, and I jumped up. We were

sitting ducks. They could drop some kind of gas or bomb in here and that would be the end of it. I ran to the ladder and looked up. At least the ship wasn't directly over the opening. That was something. Unless they'd already dropped men who would deliver the next bomb personally. Like a pod city delivery, but instead of getting thermoplastic-fiber furniture, we'd get our heads blown off.

"Put your suits on," Kale addressed his group. "The oxygen will leak out of this place fast."

Oxygen. My dad did an emergency drill with us once in case something crazy happened. I'd only been about ten years old. He'd been so sure the door would hold, he said we wouldn't need it. The memory clicked into place.

I gestured to the wall. "Everyone get back behind the table. There's a metal partition that slides out and will seal the rest of the shelter so the air doesn't escape." The only area it excluded was the front part—where the ladder and door were. And me. James hesitated but moved farther back with the others.

"Just let me back in, okay?" I yelled.

James gave me a thumbs-up, before he became obscured from my view by the wall that Kale slid across the room.

I took the ladder two rungs at a time, and peered out the hole where the door used to be. There wasn't anyone on the ground. Kale's small ship stood miraculously intact. He'd been right that they wouldn't want to waste a good ship. Its hatch door was open though, so they'd either looted it or tried to fly away with it. I hoped it was the latter and wished I could've seen their faces when they realized Kale had sabotaged their plans.

The roar of the Consulate ship caught my attention and I looked skyward. It had flown about a thousand feet away but circled back around toward the shelter. If they hadn't realized they'd succeeded in breaking in with the last bomb drop, they'd sure know it in a minute when they passed over the empty space where the door had been.

The large white ship revved its engines, blotting out the sun for one glorious moment as it sped toward me. Laser pulses shot out from the ship. They'd spotted me. I hunched close to the ground and raised B.K., waiting for the perfect shot. It was difficult ignoring the pulsing lasers as they got closer to me. The pulses crackled loudly as they hit the dirt, and the acrid smell of smoke filled my nostrils. At least there was nothing that could catch fire. Except me.

One shot came close to Kale's ship and I knew we weren't ever getting off this planet without transportation. My heart raced about a thousand beats per minute. I took a deep breath and bolted out of the doorway. I ran, dodging the death rays coming my way, until I was directly under the ship. I lifted my gun, aiming it right at the rear under-side of the ship. They must have guessed what I was doing right as I hit the trigger panel. The ship veered sharply to the left just as the laser traveled the distance to the ship. I still hit it, but not dead center in the engine like I'd planned. If it had been a perfect hit, the whole ship would have exploded.

Instead, the laser connected with the area where the right wing merged with the ship. Flames licked along the ship where I'd shot it. The ship swerved, no longer in control without the functioning wing. Huge clouds of smoke billowed out as it dropped. It hit the ground just over the ridge where Kale's ship had been last night. An explosion ripped through the air as the ship crashed, but the only thing visible over the ridge were large plumes of rising smoke. I turned to run back to the shelter and jumped when I came face-to-face with a suit. My body—already on overload—started shaking. "What are you doing out here?"

James' voice rang low and clear through the helmet coms. "I thought you might need help. I didn't know your plan was a suicide run straight at the ship."

"My plan was to save us. Remember? I did what I had to." I tried to calm myself as we went back to the shelter, but adrenaline still coursed through my body. My legs shook as I climbed back down the ladder then refused to hold me up when I hit the floor. I sank to my knees, trying to catch my breath. The metal containment wall remained shut tight on the other side of the room.

James jumped down behind me and knelt at my side. His hand pressed lightly on my lower back. "You can't fly solo all the time."

"Like I've had any choice about that," I said. I was too tired to move away from his touch.

His hand dropped as the wall slid open a foot. Kale leaned out. "Get the hell in here, you two."

James steadied me and helped me through the partition. I pulled my helmet off and took a deep breath, while Kale secured the sliding door. He turned and assessed me. "Please tell me the explosion I heard was their ship being blown to smithereens."

I inspected my feet. "Um . . . let's just say that while I didn't exactly kill their ship, it is severely injured. It crashed—that's something, right?"

Britta groaned. "Great."

Seriously? Let her try and take out a ship that size on her own. "I did the best I could. What is your deal?"

Britta opened her mouth to respond. Her gaze flicked to James and she shut it again. Finally, she sighed. "No big deal. Just sayin' it could have gone better is all."

James stared coolly at Britta. "She risked her life out there."

Kale raised an eyebrow at James, then turned to me. "You're quite the soldier. I'm impressed, Tora."

I shrugged. "They were close to hitting your ship and I wanted to save it." All heads swiveled in my direction. "I knew if the ship was compromised, we'd have no chance of getting out of here. So I thought I'd run out real quick and blow them up."

Kale laughed. Britta scoffed but otherwise remained silent.

Markus smiled like a proud parent. "I told you she was

a tough one." Then he pointed at the metal wall. "I hate to be the voice of reason, but if any of those burners lived through the crash, I'm thinking not having a door could be problematic."

He was right, nothing would stop a bomb from being thrown inside. But they'd have to be able to walk to do it.

Kale grabbed his helmet. "Britta, suit up, and guard the opening. Call me on the com if anything looks suspicious."

If you asked me, Britta was the thing that looked suspicious. But no one asked me. She glared at Kale like he was a moron. "Where the hell are you going? And why the hell aren't we just moving the guns and getting out of here?"

Kale spoke calmly, as though bringing down government ships was something he did before breakfast each day. "Because we need to make sure they're all dead. Hopefully the crash knocked out their com system and there won't be any help on the way."

"It's standard military procedure," James added. A mix of anger and sadness crossed his face as he spoke the words.

"We'll move the guns," Kale said sharply. "But we also have to salvage all spare parts we can from their ship . . . and we have to finish off any survivors. Do you think you can handle this, Britta?" His face burned with contempt and I knew he was referencing her earlier defiance.

I stared at Kale in disbelief. "You mean, if someone over there is injured, you're just going to shoot them dead? I'd hope we could be more civil than that."

Kale squared his shoulders. "Hope is for pansies who can't shoot straight."

"No enemy survivors left alive. It's protocol." James spit out the words.

Kale's voice was flat. "Trust me. They'd do the same to us."

I believed him. I mean it wasn't like the Consulate came waving peace signs at us, but I just didn't get it. With so few human survivors in existence, everyone still insisted on the "us versus them" mentality. It would probably stay that way until the last human fizzled out. Markus was right that I didn't think we deserved the chance to mess up another planet.

Britta still wore a sour expression on her face, but I'd begun to think it was the only one she had. Kale tipped Britta's chin upward. Maybe he meant it in an encouraging way, but it looked menacing to me. "Buck up, soldier. We'll be out of here soon."

Kale would go to his ship to make any necessary repairs and reinstall the fuel converter, while Britta, James, and Markus guarded the shelter door and watched for trouble.

"Oh, one more thing," Kale said before he left. He touched the device on his forearm. "I want everyone's com devices left on from here on out."

Britta looked quizzical. "Why?"

Kale seemed to weigh his response before answering. "We need to be able to hear one another at all times. What if something happens while we're separated?"

James flipped his device on immediately. "Yes, sir. Good idea."

I couldn't decide if Kale did this because he didn't trust Britta, or because he didn't trust me, but I knew for sure that it had nothing to do with his concern for our well-being. He just wanted to hear what was said at all times. Britta and Markus turned on their devices, and it made me glad I didn't have one myself.

After Kale left, I excused myself and said I needed to gather my things. This was it. I was leaving this place forever. The place I'd considered home for half my life. Memories of my family, the good and the bad, wouldn't come as easily without the familiar reminders of the shelter around me.

I only had one more chance to visit my favorite room, so I headed down the hall. Even after all this time, the presence of my father was strong in the room. The study held a feeling of safety and comfort. I sat at his work station, running my hand along the smooth surface. The desk reminded me of him. Silent and strong constitution. The contents of the desk were neat and orderly, his work space meticulous. I'd briefly riffled through his things after he died, yet felt like I was violating his privacy even in death. Color-coded tablets were stacked in one drawer. I'd looked through the secret, plastic tablets after his death, but they mainly involved notes about the bioenergetic weapons. Most people had long ago shunned notebooks in favor of energetic devices, but my father knew you couldn't hack a notebook the same way you could an e-device—the Consulate would have to physically find it first.

The last time I'd been in this room with him was the day before he left for his last Consulate meeting. He'd been in there for hours, and when I knocked on the door he hadn't answered. Worried, I'd opened the door and found him sitting at his station with his head in his hands. The tablets were spread out everywhere.

"Dad?" I'd asked. "Everything okay?"

"Come in, Tora. I want to tell you something."

The tone in his voice sounded worried and sad. I didn't detect any of the confidence he'd had when he'd taken me to the Consulate meeting in the pod city.

"Do you see these books? All my years of work are contained in them—everything about bioenergetic weapons that you'd ever want to know." He took his arm and swiped the tablets onto the floor. "And I'm ashamed of them. I wish I'd listened to my gut instead of the Consulate propaganda. I'm so sorry. You must think so little of me."

"No, Dad. I think you're so strong. It takes a lot of guts to stand up to the government." Even though I still had no clue what the Consulate intended to do with the weapons, I wasn't used to seeing Dad like this. He was usually so stoic and calm. I picked up the tablets and set them on the edge of the station.

He reached out and gave me an awkward pat on the arm. "Thank you. Remember how strong you are, Tora. Don't ever forget that, no matter how hard things are."

I smiled and put my arm around him. "Come on, Dad. We have a dying sun and barely any air or water. How much worse could things get?"

If I'd only known at the time. I picked up a random tablet and leafed through it. It wouldn't be good to leave these behind. This one contained detailed descriptions about how to rekey a trigger panel to a different vibration. Pages of equations filled other pages. Equations I didn't understand, nor wanted to, but knew they'd be of interest to the Consulate. Not that I wanted to bring the tablets with me either. Too easy for them to fall into enemy hands—or Kale's. I wasn't sure which option was worse. I decided I'd use the natural resources around me to my advantage. I'd burn them.

When I set the stack of tablets atop the desk, one stood out, different than the rest. The one that I'd stuffed deep in the drawer because the sight of it caused me pain. Instead of a red, yellow, or green color, it was mauve. My mother's journal. She had to have been the only person left in the world that still used a diary. She'd started using it after we'd moved to the bunker, after she'd become a ghost of her former self. She kept it mostly to herself, hidden, which I guess was the point. I found it after Dad died and thought reading it might help me understand the great sadness she carried. The first few pages broke my heart so much that I couldn't go on. I'd put it away where it couldn't hurt me anymore.

I gripped the edges of the notebook, and forced myself

to uncurl my fingers and open the cover. I lifted the pages to my nose, inhaling, desperate for a trace of my mother's scent. All I smelled were the plastic pages.

My mother's loose sentences flowed along the pages, tangential ramblings about her fears and shattered dreams. Nothing about hope or love. Before I knew it, tears dripped from my eyes onto her words. It was just pain and more pain—no wonder I'd stopped reading. I wiped my face in frustration and flipped to the last page of the book. Instead of my mother's large, looped writing I found my father's small, blockish handwriting. I looked up to the date at the top of the page and slammed the book shut.

It was the date of my mother's and sister's death.

Chapter FOURTEEN

I SHOVED THE BOOK DEEP INTO THE BAG, NEXT TO THE MEDS, like that could distance me from whatever truth it contained. Truth that I wasn't sure I wanted to face. Memories of my mother, begging my father for more pain meds, crying late into the night. Memories of my sister's light laughter as she danced just out of reach. If I read any more of the journal right now, I'd fall apart, which was something I couldn't afford to do. Maybe the day would come that I'd be ready, if I lived that long, but today was not that day.

"Get the hell out here, Tora. We're packing for survival, not an intergalactic vacation."

I marched down the hall with my bag over my shoulder and the stacks of scientific notebooks in my arms. "For your information, Markus, I was going through important documents." Then I realized that their com systems were on, and I didn't want Kale to know about the existence of the gun journals.

A sharp rapping echoed on the metal wall and Britta stumbled inside when he opened it. She tore off her helmet and threw it on the floor at Markus' feet. "Your turn, big guy, it's so burnin' hot up there I'm about to pass out."

Despite her whining, she managed to smile at him, and he grinned at her. "Don't worry, baby. I got it covered."

Baby? Just when I thought they couldn't get any worse.

He patted her ass as he went past her. She blew him a kiss before securing the wall behind him.

James looked up at me from the table. "Hey, can I talk to you a sec?"

I shifted the tablets in my hand. The book burning could wait another minute. I nodded toward my room, and he pushed his chair back slowly and walked toward me. My stomach started doing somersaults.

I led James into my room and put the books on the floor before turning to face him. He took a step toward me and kicked the door shut with his foot. Even his method of shutting doors was hot. "Before we leave, I just thought I should get a look at those ribs. Make sure they're healing okay."

My hopes deflated. "Seriously?" Maybe I'd only imagined that time in the weapons room. "Uh, sure. Okay." I shifted my satchel over to the other side, and lifted my shirt up a little.

James took his fingers and gently pressed on my rib cage. "Does that hurt?" he asked.

"No." My eyes focused on the wall in front of me. I was not going to look at him.

"Not even a little?"

Did I detect a note of urgency in his voice? I forced myself to look at him, and his eyes seared into mine. I didn't know what he wanted me to say. The crackle of his com device reminded me we weren't really alone. I tried to focus on his voice.

"Um, maybe a little right there," I said.

He moved closer to me, until our faces were inches apart. Still staring at me, he moved his hand down lower over my ribs. Electric tingles shot through me as he ran his hand back up my rib cage and traced the highest rib from the outside toward my sternum. His touch was soft but sure. His eyes were what got me. They looked vulnerable, like they did when we were in the weapons room. If this was all an act, he deserved a prize, because I was beginning to buy it.

Our lips were so close that I felt his breath in my mouth as his fingers continued to caress my body. My body shuddered under his hand.

"How 'bout here? Does it hurt when I touch here?" he asked in a professional tone, but both his hands slid down toward my hips and his lips almost touched mine. I was no doctor but this was definitely not part of any medical exam I'd ever seen. My legs turned to jelly and I trembled. When

I sighed, James raised a finger to his lips. Oh yeah, the com system.

"Um, no. Just a little tenderness there but I think I'll be okay," I lied. I might never be okay again, knowing how his hands could make my body react. Not that I minded him speaking through his hands, but I wished he could also use words.

Words. My eyes fell on the stack of books on the floor, and I pointed at them. He nodded and grabbed one, while still talking about my injury in clinical tones.

He handed me one of the books and kept his hand on my arm, while I dug for a writing instrument in the satchel. My body burned in a way it never had before. Maybe some feelings weren't so bad after all.

I found my e-pen and flipped open a page, while James coughed to mask the sound. *How come you can fire the guns too?* I wrote, while I asked aloud about my estimated recovery period. His hand felt like fire on my arm.

I have no idea. I was hoping you could tell me. He paused, then scribbled quickly as he spoke about the projected healing time of a fractured rib. *What's your sister's name?* He handed back the pen.

My hand froze. I hadn't spoken her name since I was ten years old. It was painful enough referring to her as my little sister. Her name might rip me into a thousand little pieces. I'd been afraid all these years that saying her name aloud might kill me. Guess writing it might be easier. *Callie.*

He twisted the e-pen from my hand and left his fingers

twined with mine a minute before he started writing again. *My sister's name was Autumn. Even though the only season we've known is summer, my sister dreamed of leaves. Like Callie and her flowers.*

I grabbed the pen again. *They would have gotten along great.* I knew what else I needed to know. *Why so loyal to Kale?*

James paused and his face looked darker when he began writing again. *Kale is part of something bigger. I have to make sure—*

"James!" Kale's voice filled the room and I gasped.

"Sir?" James clicked the button on his com device.

"I need you over here pronto to help with some parts."

James rolled his eyes at me. "Got it. I'll be right there." He brushed my cheek with the back of his hand, in stark contrast to his businesslike tone. "Well, Tora, this looks as good as can be expected. Just let me know if you have any pain or discomfort. Okay?"

"Got it." He stared into my eyes a second longer, before he took off to help Kale.

I exhaled slowly and attempted to regain my composure. The way I felt when he was near scared me, and I didn't like to be scared. I reached down to grab the books and carried the stack into the front room, where Britta was busy sucking down some Caelia Pure.

"Let me in!" Markus yelled through the door. I opened it, helmet and books in hand, as he sauntered by me.

"Be back in a second," I said and slipped through the opening.

Markus frowned. "Where do you think you're going?"

I slid the door shut behind me.

"Hey—"

I ignored Markus' protests and made my way up the ladder with the notebooks. Once outside, I placed the stack of tablets on the ground then stepped back ten paces. The sun would take care of them by itself, but I wanted to speed up the process. I removed B.K. from my waist, set it to burn, and took aim.

I pressed the button and the books erupted in flames, the smell of burned plastic wafting through the air. Hundreds of hours of my father's work incinerated in an instant. A small pang of guilt hit me, but I shrugged it off. Though my father hadn't intended it, his notes could be used to rekey the guns to any vibration. I couldn't let that happen. Satisfied, I went back down and pounded on the emergency door.

Markus looked down at my now empty hands with a questioning eye. "Did you just shoot tablets? Because I really didn't figure you for the book-burning type."

I shrugged and kept walking past him and Britta, who just stared at me. "Just let me know when Kale and James get back," I called over my shoulder.

I wanted some alone time. Once inside my room, I pulled up the ocean on my Infinity. My sister and I used to lie side by side looking at the screen, pretending we were on a family vacation.

Your pink swimsuit looks muy bonita *on you,* she would

tell me, her seven-year-old voice mimicking an adult. We felt like rebels using Spanish now that it was supposed to be extinct too. Gracias, I'd respond, *now let's collect seashells in your purple bucket.* It was a stupid game but it made us happy at a time when little else did. My father was always in his study and my mother . . . well, she was never happy.

I closed down the picture and opened the GlobalNet. Still no signs of life. *Qué sorpresa.* I'd neglected Surviving Burn Out the past two days. I tapped my fingers across the keyboard that had appeared in front of me. What to discuss? Coming under enemy fire by our own government? Admit to my vast readership that there is no surviving burn out—that death is the only real escape? Unless you can find a group of burners who want to "rescue" you so they can use you for your guns.

I didn't notice the blinking light coming from the bottom of the screen at first. I'd never seen it before. Green and flashing rapidly. What the hell was it? It wasn't like the battery could run low since it was powered by my own energy. I took my finger and scrolled down until my finger waved over the light. A caption popped up from the screen into the air in front of me. It was attached to my chronically recycled post.

My first comment.

Chapter FIFTEEN

*HEY—JUST FOUND THIS ON THE NET. I'M ALEC. I'M SEVEN-
teen. I'm the only one left in Sector 2. Maybe the only one
left anywhere, aside from you. Please respond if you're still
there . . .* por favor.

There was another survivor out there, and he knew
Spanish. The *por favor* added a note of desperation to the
almost nonchalant tone of the rest of the message. I called
up a map to look at the sectors. Geography didn't matter
much when every zone was a dead one. Sector 2 looked
to be about where Australia was before the final drought
when the government restructured everything into sectors. When I started to type a reply, a new box came up,
saying he was on GlobalNet and ready to chat.

Alec? I typed hesitantly.

The response was almost instant. *Damn. I thought it was too good to be true.*

My heart almost stopped in my chest. Though I'd faithfully posted on the Net each week, it felt like I'd been writing into a void. I'd stopped believing that I'd actually find a fellow survivor.

I'm here. I'm Tora.

My finger hovered over the send button, when my cynical side took over. I typed rapidly.

How do I know you're not really a poser from the Consulate pretending to be a survivor?

A long pause stretched into what seemed like eternity before I heard back. The string of expletives he wrote back about the Consulate told me he was either an excellent liar or he really hated them.

Alec typed fast and furious. He told me that his family was poor—too poor for a pod city, and he'd only gotten lucky when he found a GlobalNet device in a dead family's pod. He said Sector 2's pod city actually had a name—Consulate City. Wow, they were as creative with their names as I was with my guns.

He'd lived on the outskirts of that city like we did here, meaning no dome for protection. Only single pod units with unreliable air and water systems. When those systems broke down, you either had to have money to fix it or you'd be toast. Literally. It was just him and his dad, until their water system began failing and their pleas for assistance were ignored by the government. Alec woke one morning to find a note from his dad saying he'd gone to demand help from the Consulate. Knowing that the Consulate wouldn't help, he ran to a friend's house. They didn't have enough water as it was, but agreed to let him stay.

The guilt over not going after his father burned his insides more than the sun ever could.

Several weeks later, his friend's home was stormed by the Consulate. Alec had grabbed an old sunsuit and hidden in a crawl space under the pod, but heard them murder his friend and his friend's family.

I shook my head. It didn't make sense.

Why? What did your friend's family do wrong?

A long moment passed.

Nothing. The Consulate wanted the W.A.R. It was the only thing missing when I went back inside.

I didn't understand.

Why would the government want a W.A.R. machine?

Alec wrote that he heard times were getting tough, even inside the pod cities, and the Consulate was looking for excuses to take the machines from the poor. A new planet hadn't been found yet and even the government panicked. They started out just taking W.A.R.'s from the families of the deceased, and created a law that it was illegal to be in possession of a W.A.R. machine that wasn't yours. So many people outside the cities took W.A.R.'s from the dead, but since they were government-issued, the Consulate knew who was registered to have one and who wasn't. If you didn't give it back, they killed you.

Alec continued typing at a rapid pace.

I think when the situation in the city became more desperate, they stopped waiting for people to die off and started taking the machines by force. The Consulate probably thought they were doing them a favor by killing them outright, instead of letting them die slowly of dehydration. I heard them accuse my friend's family of treason, though I think that was a bunch of shit.

I knew the government had killed my father, but killing innocent children was unbelievable. I shuddered.

So a trumped-up treason charge helps those burners feel better about murdering people?

He responded:

Don't you get it, Tora? Treason makes them the enemy. No enemy survivors. Which really means no witnesses. Trust me, if they knew I'd been hiding out, they would have killed me too—then there'd be no survivor in my sector. I heard them marching up and down the pod streets, and the only sound was gun blasts.

He'd only survived because he found a hidden W.A.R. machine under a pod. Alec's words sent a chill up my spine. No enemy survivors. Both Kale and James had referred to that earlier. Had James experienced something like that with the Consulate? I couldn't work out how Kale figured into everything, or how James and Kale were connected.

My father's genius was a mixed blessing. He'd created super-guns, but also had been able to restructure our W.A.R. machine to accommodate the drop in atmospheric water particles. The government didn't have my father's brains. It made sense that if they couldn't make their existing W.A.R.

machines more sensitive, they needed more of them to harvest enough water to survive. And they believed that their lives were of greater importance than those of the "lower class" citizens outside the cities. My dad's super-weapons would have killed people faster and more efficiently than having to shoot multiple lasers at each person. And if they got lucky and found a planet, which they did, the guns would provide order in the new world.

My fingers flew across the keyboard, telling Alec that if I wasn't killed by the assholes I was living with, I'd find a way to get there and rescue him. I also mentioned that I noticed his Spanish and loved the language. We logged off and I promised to rescue him if I survived. His parting words gave me hope.

Buena suerte, *Tora. You're pretty damn strong if you made it this far.*

I went back into the front room just as James and Kale signaled their return with a knock on the sliding door. I'd decided not to tell any of them about Alec yet. I hadn't figured out how to play that card.

"How'd it go?" I asked James, trying to sound casual.

He wouldn't meet my eyes.

"Got her all fixed up." Kale's pride in the ship was evident. "She's good to go, as soon as we load her with the ammo and visit our friends over yonder." He motioned his head in the direction of the crash.

James continued to stare at some imaginary spot on the wall. Something was wrong.

Britta stared back and forth between them, then jerked her thumb at me. "This one's been busy too—shooting books." Britta fake coughed into her arm as she muttered "crazy bitch." Yet her tone was different, not as evil as usual.

I pulled my shoulders back and stood upright. "Yes, I shot them. They sure won't be bothering us again anytime soon. You got any questions?"

Kale studied me, his expression unreadable. "That explains the pile of ash out there." He turned to address the group. "All right, people. Listen up. We'll do what we did before and fly between the night storms." Kale's voice projected confidence and control. "Unless we find survivors, it's purely a salvage mission. Then, on to Caelia."

"Don't forget where you promised to take me when we get there," James said.

Good thing he wasn't being cryptic or anything.

Kale waved his hand in the air. "Yeah, yeah, of course. A soldier never breaks a promise."

The way Kale strode around the small space, his leg pain must have significantly receded, because his gait was almost normal. He hadn't asked for any more pain meds either.

James' eyes were glued to my sister's wildflower painting like it was the most astounding masterpiece he'd ever come across. Definitely avoiding eye contact. What had changed? If only I could get him alone, but he wasn't veering far from Kale's side. I patted my satchel, the weight of

The Obliterator providing strange comfort. James was the only one who knew T.O. existed, and whatever was going on with him, I didn't think he would have told Kale.

I stood and crossed the room to remove my sister's picture from the wall, then carefully placed it in my satchel. I gave up trying to catch James' eyes and situated myself in a chair. Fine. I just had to hope that even if it didn't seem like it, that moment in my room was real.

Kale cleared his throat. "Helmets on everyone. Let's move some guns."

Any ideas I had about finding alone time with James were shattered when he refused to come within ten feet of me. Instead, he and Britta grabbed a box of guns and followed Kale up the ladder. Frustrated, I leaned down and hauled up one of the remaining boxes. Being alone wasn't new, so James' behavior shouldn't have stung so much.

Markus came up behind me and grabbed the bottom edge of the box. "Here, let me help you."

Tears sprang to my eyes and I blinked them away. Maybe he couldn't tell through the helmet. "I'm fine, Markus. I don't need help." I tried to lift the box higher so it would cover my face.

He pulled the box out of my arms with ease and set it on the floor, then yanked off his helmet. He made a show of turning off the com device on his arm.

I pulled my helmet off and shook my head. "You're going to get in trouble for that—"

"Look, I've wanted to talk to you alone but haven't had

the chance. I'm sorry for how this all went down. I don't regret much, but I regret this. Not that it matters now I guess, but I wanted you to know."

I wanted to hate Markus for everything he'd done but it would have been a waste of energy that I didn't have. I'd known him longer than any person still living in this world. "Good to know. Now do you want to tell me what the hell is going on with Britta?"

Markus laughed. "She's not that bad. Reminds me of you actually. I like my girls with a little spunk."

"The fact that you just compared me to her makes me feel ill." I studied him. "You really like her?"

He shrugged. "I kinda do. There's a side to her you haven't seen."

I raised my hand to stop him. "I don't even want to know."

Markus grinned.

The others might be wondering what was taking so long. I grabbed my helmet. "We should get over there. And turn your com device back on before Kale notices." If he hadn't already.

Markus picked up his helmet. "I just want you to know that you're not as alone as you think. I have your back." He clicked his com device back on, winked at me, and lugged the box upward.

I watched him disappear out of the opening and sighed. If only I could believe him. I bent over and ran my hands through my hair, then twisted it up to fit under the helmet.

Several boxes of guns remained, so I grabbed the lightest one and headed up. James could haul his ass back in the scorching heat to get the rest for all I cared.

Sweat dripped down me as soon as I stepped outside. Markus had already reached Kale's ship, and I cursed my slow pace but had to keep the box from hitting against my ribs. I couldn't wait to get away from this forsaken place. I still needed to figure out how to take Alec with us because I couldn't leave someone here alone to die—I knew exactly how desperate he felt. Just as I reached Kale's ship, James and Kale were exiting to head back to the bunker.

"How many left?" Kale asked me through the helmet com as they passed.

I glanced at James, who looked away. I resisted the urge to scream through the com just to get a reaction from him. "Two, and they're really heavy. Don't sweat too much." I stormed onto Kale's ship and dropped the box on the floor in the loading area. After taking off my helmet, I kicked it across the floor.

I looked up to find Britta staring at me wide-eyed from across the room. Markus watched me with concern and motioned me over. He turned his com device off again, and Britta followed suit.

I stomped over to them. "Markus, I'm fine. You need to stop doing that or—"

"You're not fine, Tora." Markus spoke quickly. "I just

went to take a piss, and James and Kale walked by in the hallway. They were talking and must not have known I was in there."

I frowned. "And?"

Markus' voice cracked. "This makes no sense at all, but Kale asked James to kill you."

My stomach dropped to the floor and my knees buckled. Britta looked whiter than I'd seen her. I looked back and forth between her and Markus. "And?"

Britta's voice came out in a whisper. "James said yes."

Chapter SIXTEEN

MY BLOOD TURNED TO ICE. I BACKED AWAY FROM THEM. IF they were telling the truth, then the first boy I'd started to fall for had turned out to be a psychopath.

Markus glanced out the window of Kale's ship. There was no sign of them yet, so they were still down in the bunker. "Whatever you think we should do, we should do it quick," he noted.

What was I supposed to do? I thought about how my family would deal with this. My sister would try and hug her way out of it, my mom would dope herself up with meds to avoid dealing with it, and my dad would try to have a rational, calm conversation with them and explain his position. None of those options gave me a chance in hell of getting out alive.

"Do you know how to fly this bird?" I asked Markus.

Markus looked sheepish. "Yeah, I'm the copilot."

"So let's fly it then."

Britta shrieked and pointed out the window. "They're coming back."

Kale and James each carried a box of Dad's guns. It made me glad I left the heaviest ones for them so it would slow them down. The sight of James caused a sick feeling in the pit of my stomach.

"Run!" yelled Markus, and we raced full speed toward the cockpit.

We reached the front of the ship faster than I thought possible given my ribs. Britta and I strapped ourselves in, while Markus jumped into the pilot's chair and flipped several buttons. The engine roared to life. Britta's fingers were white from gripping the arm of her seat. At least I wasn't the only terrified person in the room.

Markus flicked on his com device. "Might as well let them give me an earful."

An idea formed in my head. "Okay, but don't tell them you overheard their plan."

A second later, Kale's voice boomed through his com system. "What the hell? I didn't give orders to start her up. Report, soldier."

Markus gave me a questioning look but I shook my head. He pulled back on the throttle and the ship lifted and turned. James and Kale had dropped the guns and ran directly toward us. Kale lifted his own weapon and aimed at the ship—his ship. A leaden weight sank in my stomach. I hadn't planned on the fact that he'd be willing to try and take down his own ship.

"Oh, God. He's gonna shoot us down!" Britta screamed and covered her eyes with her hands.

James reached over and put his hand on top of Kale's gun, pushing it down toward the ground. Some exchange took place and then it was James' voice I heard through Markus' com. "Tora, what are you doing?"

The deep scratchiness of his voice got to me, even through the com device.

"Keep going," I told Markus. "And toss me your com device."

We had to be almost out of firing range. If James had really wanted me dead, why did he stop Kale from shooting us? Unless what he wanted in one piece wasn't me, but the ship and my guns.

Once I had the com device in my hand, I wanted to rage at him for betraying my trust and tell him where he could put those guns, but I also knew what he must be thinking. That I'd left them to die down there. Now he'd know how I felt. But a part of me wondered if maybe Kale was the one James was deceiving. I refused to believe that the time in the weapons room and my room had all been an act. Or maybe I was just refusing to believe what a bad judge of character I really was. I fiddled with the device.

"Tora?"

"I'm here. Give me a sec." I clicked off the device.

"Hey, Tora?" Markus asked.

Irritated, I looked up. "What?"

"Are we out for a joyride or are we actually going somewhere? Like Caelia. Just wondering if I'm supposed to be headed in a specific direction is all."

I shook my head. "Not Caelia. Sector Two."

Shock crossed Britta's face. "But there's nothing there. It's a giant dust bowl, just like here. Come on, I want off this burnin' planet."

"Yeah," Markus agreed. "What's up?"

"There's a survivor there. I promised I'd help him if I could. So we're helping."

Markus nodded. "Another survivor? Cool." He entered coordinates and flicked a switch, which must have set some type of autopilot, because he stretched his arms above his head. "So, to Sector Two. In and out, and on to Caelia, right?"

I frowned. That plan made the most sense, but leaving James and Kale meant they'd die for sure. It made me no better than them, not that I wanted to be the one dying either. If there was even a chance James was playing Kale, could I live with the fact that I'd killed them? At least by rescuing Alec, I'd have someone to back me up if we did go back and I was wrong about James.

"Right. Maybe. Well, n-no. We might go back for them." I pressed the button on the com device. "You still there?"

The pause felt like an eternity. "Yeah, I'm still here." His voice sent tingles along my spine. How could I spin this so Kale wouldn't suspect that I'd caught wind of his plan to kill me, yet still make our sudden exit believable? Maybe I'd give the truth a shot.

"There's another survivor. In Sector Two. I knew Kale wouldn't agree to save him, that he'd think one life wasn't worth deviating from the plan. I think one life is worth something."

Nothing but silence from the other end. My heart pounded. "Anyway, we're going to get him. It'll only take a few hours and we'll be back for you. Then we'll ship out."

Several choice curse words erupted through the line. Kale was not a happy camper. He must have grabbed the com system from James. "You've got buckets to learn about being a soldier, soldier. You better have your asses back here by sixteen hundred hours. Meet us at the Consulate ship."

Oh, that's right—the "no enemy survivors" thing.

"We'll be there." I clicked off and took in a huge breath. I had no idea what I'd do when we got there, but hopefully, I'd figure something out. At least it sounded like Kale bought my story. My insubordination would be attributed to being a bleeding heart rather than running from him.

I tossed the device back to Markus. "You must both think I'm crazy, huh?"

Markus chuckled. "Being crazy is how you've survived this long on your own. I get us rescuing the survivor, but not sure I get the going back part. You understand they were planning to kill you, right? I don't trust Kale as far as I can throw him."

Britta studied me closely, not saying anything.

I sighed. "Go on, Britta. Just say what you're thinking. At least I know you won't sugarcoat it."

She chewed her nail. "Look, I'm already on Kale's shit list and he'll probably blame this on me too. Markus is right that I don't think we can trust Kale anymore. But the James thing . . ."

"What?"

Britta spit off part of her nail. "It's just that, for whatever reason, I think he likes you . . . or liked you anyway. Just something he said while you were out of the room in the bunker. That I should lay off you . . . that you could be trusted."

My heart raced. "You waited to tell me this until now?"

She shrugged. "Does it matter? He still told Kale he'd kill you. You know the score as well as I do. It's kill or be killed. That's why we're both survivors."

Kill or be killed. It was sad that entire human existence had been reduced to such a bleak motto. But it was true.

"But what if James didn't mean it and was just playing along?" I heard the desperation in my voice.

"Maybe," Britta agreed, "but are you gonna risk being blasted into bits just to find that out?"

She had a point.

Britta's face changed. She looked lost in thought. After a minute, her eyes refocused on me. "You're not the only one that's been burned by someone you trusted. It sucks, but you know, what doesn't kill you . . ."

"Makes you one tough-ass bitch," Markus finished. He blew Britta a kiss. "I'll take care of you, baby. I promise I won't take my eyes off you."

Britta tossed her hair over her shoulder. "And what if I want more than your eyes on me?"

Ewwww.

Markus smirked. "It's on autopilot and we've got a little time to kill." He sauntered over to Britta and laced his fingers through hers. "Come with me, beautiful."

I gawked at them. "What? You can't leave me up here by myself. What if something goes wrong?"

He laughed and pulled Britta through the doorway. "Get some rest. You look exhausted. If any alarms go off, you know where to find me."

The sky zoomed by at an amazing speed, and though I'd never traveled to this part of the world before, it was hard to ignore the fact that Markus and Britta were doing god-knows-what in the other room.

I typed a quick message to Alec letting him know we were on the way, and he messaged back that he was "in awe of my bad-assedness." I had a sneaking suspicion that he had an addiction to old shows too.

After a while, I refused to look down at the ground below. It was too depressing. The devastation reached everywhere. Miles upon miles of rock and dirt stretched before the ship, punctuated by the occasional cacti grove. The cacti were the only evidence that the planet wasn't completely dead.

I must have drifted off for awhile, and I woke with my right hand gripping the Infinity on my wrist. I fingered the device, trying to figure out what the hell I could do to save myself when we returned to the Consulate ship. Hoping Kale and James wouldn't try to ambush me, hoping I wouldn't have to kill people, hoping there was still a peaceful way out of this mess. Kale's voice echoed in my head: *Hope is for pansies who can't shoot straight.*

A noise sounded near me and I whipped my head around.

Markus grinned. "You were expecting someone else?"

Britta followed him. I noted her mussed hair and strange facial expression. It took me a minute to realize she was smiling, a real smile, not the sideways ones I'd seen before.

Markus settled into the pilot chair and pulled Britta onto his lap. She curled her body around his, resting her head on his shoulder. I threw up in my mouth a little bit, but refrained from issuing a flight safety lecture about multiple occupants in the pilot's space.

Markus stroked Britta's hair. "I hope you slept as well as we did."

I rolled my eyes. "Is that what you call what you were doing?"

Markus laughed but it died quickly. He stared at me. "So, here's what I don't get. You're the only one who can fire the guns, so why would Kale want you dead?"

I wasn't ready to disclose that James could fire them

too, though Kale had to know. Because James told him. Kale wouldn't want me dead unless he knew of another way to fire the weapons.

"Maybe the guns aren't as important to him now and he just wants me out of the way?"

"No way," said Britta. "Guns are always important to Kale. But the Consulate wants someone who can fire them, so killing you doesn't add up. I mean, James is smart and all, but it's not like he knows how to reprogram a gun. There's something else going on."

I got that. I just couldn't figure out why James would be part of it. "How well do you know James anyway?"

Britta leaned into Markus. "We met when we both broke into the same abandoned pod trying to steal the W.A.R. machine. I could tell he really wanted it, needed it, but he let me have it . . . said he'd get one from another pod." She smiled at the memory. "I thought he was decent. Anyway, we exchanged information and I told him I'd heard about a former government soldier who knew what the Consulate was doing with the W.A.R. machines. We decided to find him."

"Kale."

Britta nodded. "Yep."

It still didn't explain why James would want to kill me. "James certainly seems loyal to Kale."

Britta frowned. "That's what I don't get. Yes, he's loyal to him . . . for a lot of reasons. But I still don't understand the killing you part. I don't know what's going on. The fact that they seem to have some new secret agenda is bad for all of us. 'Cept Markus. Kale wants him since his last copilot got skewered by that cactus."

I eyed Markus. "What about you? Wanna tell me how you got hooked up with Kale in the first place?"

Markus squirmed a bit under Britta. "The first time I came to see you, I really thought you'd come with me and we'd sell the guns to the highest bidder." He laughed. "Stupid me. Anyway, when I got back to Caelia, I heard about Kale's interest in the guns and searched him out. He contacted the Consulate . . . and well, you know the rest. He's a burner."

A wave of fresh anger rode through me. "That didn't seem to bother you much when you thought you were getting paid. Kale might need a copilot but he was ready to shoot you down in this ship along with me."

Markus took his hands off Britta and held them palms up toward me. "I said I'm sorry. I have no doubt he'll kill whoever he wants to, or thinks he has to."

Britta shifted in Markus' lap. "Kale looks at me like I've defied orders one too many times. For him, that's enough to make someone the enemy." She bit her nail again in quick, jagged movements. "Don't get me wrong, if this had gone down a day ago, hell, even a few hours ago, I would have jumped at the chance to take you down." Britta looked down at the ground. "But . . . it looks like we're both on Kale's bad side right now."

Yeah, I remembered some old saying: *The enemy of my enemy is my friend.* I thought about it. Kale had a crate of super-weapons, and someone who could fire them. He had what he needed, aside from a functioning ship.

I had Markus, who despite some significant character defects, had warned me about Kale and gotten me out of there. He'd backed up his words about having my back, and since he and Britta seemed to care about each other—which I might never understand—she might be less likely to jump me again. And we had the ship.

I narrowed my eyes at Britta. "But don't you owe your life to Kale too?"

Britta trailed her finger along Markus' arm. "Kale did save my life, and I owe him for that. I took this job because he promised me a lot of money—said I could start my life over on Caelia once it was finished. That doesn't look like it's going to happen. So I'm grateful to him, but I'm not going to be anyone's puppet."

She smiled at Markus again, and I guessed the rest. He'd made her promises that were better than Kale's. Promises that twisted the bitterness she wore so well into something that looked almost like happiness. Something in my gut twisted inside. They had something I didn't. Whatever I thought I had with James was delusion on my part. I had no one. I was alone.

Markus patted her leg and Britta rose from his lap. "We're almost there. I gotta land this bird." He winked at me. "I understand why you want to go back. If we stick together, we can deal with Kale."

I nodded even though I wasn't sure what we could do to stop them.

Britta flashed me her version of a smile. "Don't worry. I'm too badass for them to mess with."

Markus smirked and smacked her butt. "You lost me at 'ass.' What was the rest?"

She swatted his hand away, laughing.

I fake coughed into my hand. "Gross."

Markus guided the ship down. "Here it is. Sector Two."

The dome sat on the ground, looking like a curved bit of plastic had been plopped in the midst of nowhere. It looked exactly like the one in Sector 5, from what I remembered. How ironic that he couldn't make it inside the pod city until everyone else left. It wasn't until we'd almost touched down that I noticed the things clustered by the pod city's main entrance.

"What are those piles out there by the door?" I asked.

No one answered. The ship touched down and I reached for my helmet. As we got closer, the piles came into focus—bodies. They were people who had tried to get into the dome and been burned to ash. My head swam.

Markus spoke up. "They're outside our dome too. I'd imagine the numbers were much higher than this . . . the winds would have blown away most of them."

A sick feeling knotted inside my stomach. These people were banging on the door, begging to be let in, and the Consulate let them all roast in their sunsuits. If anyone deserved the wrong end of my father's weapons, it was those burners.

"Don't think about it too much," said Britta. "Sadness just slows you down."

My thoughts exactly. Maybe we were more alike than I'd realized. We trudged the short distance to the door with our guns powered up, just in case. I kept my eyes straight ahead, ignoring the carcasses littering the perimeter of the entrance.

The door opened easily enough now that the place was empty. The streets were deserted. Rows of empty pod houses lined the streets. It reminded me of the hide-and-seek dream I had about my sister.

"Creepy," Britta said.

"He said he'd be in the first building on the right," I said through the helmet com.

Britta turned to look at me through her faceplate. "You sure this isn't some kind of trap?"

"Yeah, how well do you know this guy?" Markus added.

"No, I'm not sure. I'm not sure of anything anymore. It's not like we don't have guns." I shook B.K. in the air to prove my point. I didn't tell them about T.O. hiding in my bag.

Markus stopped five paces in front of me. "This is the first building on the right. I guess we go in."

I pushed past him. "I'll go first. It was my idea, right?" No one argued with me as I knocked, then opened the door to the pod building.

"Hello. Alec? Anyone here?" I called through the empty front hall. Britta and Markus followed behind, their guns drawn.

We cautiously removed our helmets and the oxygen seemed okay in here. I moved a few more steps before hearing something. Footsteps. Quick ones. Too quick.

A big, furry thing rounded the corner and headed straight for me. Britta squealed in fright, and I aimed the gun in its direction. My mind raced to sort through the catalog of creatures I'd seen on the GlobalNet. This one flew at me and would reach me in seconds. I didn't have time to think. I positioned the beam at its head and moved my finger to the firing panel.

"No, don't shoot! It's harmless." I jerked my head up to see a guy running down the hall. I hoped it was Alec. He yelled again. "Stop!"

The thing was almost on top of me. "What the hell is this thing?"

He looked sheepish. "*Perro*. Lucy. She's a dog."

Chapter SEVENTEEN

LUCY-THE-DOG JUMPED ON ME, LICKING ME AS FAST AS SHE could. I jerked back and gaped at the dark-haired boy in front of me. "Is she trying to eat me?"

He laughed. "No, she likes you." He looked around at us. "Sorry, I'm Alec, obviously. Are you Tora?"

I nodded, while Markus and Britta introduced themselves. Lucy nudged my hand with her head. "I don't get it. What is she doing?"

"She wants you to pet her."

"I'm sorry. Pet her?"

"Yeah, like this." Alec walked over and ran his hand down Lucy's head and back. "Who's a good girl? Yes, you're a good girl." Lucy's tail wagged like she was on drugs. Alec smiled at me and stepped away. "Go ahead. You try."

Britta and Markus watched in stunned silence. I put my hand on Lucy, patting her awkwardly on the head a few times. This was beyond surreal. All the animals were supposed to be dead. "She's soft," I managed.

Alec smiled down at the dog. "Yeah, she's a real sweetheart." He beamed at me. "You, Tora, have no idea how happy I am to see you." His lilting accent caught me off guard. When Alec gripped me in an unexpected hug, I gasped, staring at him with my mouth wide open. The last person who had hugged me was my sister. Who was this guy?

I tried not to stare at him while he answered Markus' questions about how he'd survived on his own. His black hair and dark eyes were a complete contrast to James', which was a plus. I didn't want to think about James. He seemed very sure of himself, even his hug had been confident—and strong.

Britta inched her way over to Lucy and reached out a tentative hand. The dog slurped her tongue across the back of it.

"Ugh!" Britta wiped her hand on her sunsuit, but bent over again to touch the dog.

Alec looked uncomfortable. "Sorry for not telling you ahead of time. I was afraid you wouldn't take her if you knew."

"Wait, back up a second," said Markus. "You think we're taking that thing with us?"

Alec stood straighter. "Yeah. It's the last animal alive

down here, so I'd say we're taking her. Trust me, she's more loyal than any person you've ever met."

I stared into Lucy's deep brown eyes and watched her tail wag forcefully in response to Britta's hand on her long golden fur. She certainly seemed happier than any person I'd met. I wasn't sure what the dog had to be happy about, but I guess she wouldn't know that she was the last of her kind around.

I reached down to touch her again, but had to jostle with Britta for petting space. "How is this possible? I'd heard rumors that a few animals and plants were kept in secret by the Consulate, but we've never seen any of them in Sector Five."

Alec sighed. "Yeah, most of the animals died out a hundred or so years ago, but the Consulate kept a few species alive in case they ever found a new planet. When the water problem got worse, I heard they put most of the animals down to conserve water—you wouldn't believe how much this one drinks." He pointed at Lucy. "Don't worry though," he rushed on, "I have plenty of water and energy packets for her." He gestured at a bulging duffel bag. "Like I said, I'm the only one here and I'm a great scavenger. Everything left behind is mine, well, ours now."

Markus still stayed far from the dog. "And you got her how?"

Grief crossed Alec's face. "When I realized everyone left, I started checking out all the buildings. I broke into a Consulate building one day, and they had this huge area with metal holding cells. Most were empty but a few had animals in them." His jaw tightened and his fists clenched. "They weren't alive. Looked starved to death . . . like they were just left there. I heard whimpering and found Lucy in the last cell. She was emaciated and really dehydrated, but I got her healthy again. She was the only one alive."

Britta scratched behind Lucy's ear, and Lucy licked Britta's arm in response. Britta didn't pull away this time. "So sad. She's a pretty cool little creature. Do you know if the Consulate took any with them to Caelia? James and I didn't see any, but we only stayed in one colony."

Alec shook his head. "No clue. With how much those jerks screwed everything up, I'm surprised they made it there at all."

"Speaking of Caelia, we should head back and get the others so we can show Tora and Alec the wonder of oceans," Markus said.

Alec flashed a lopsided grin. "*Sí*. I plan on jumping into one as soon as I can." He turned toward Lucy and his eyes darkened. "And then I'm going to find me some Consulate burners and see how they like being put down."

His anger was raw and bitter—it reminded me of my own after my sister died.

Britta nodded. "I'll definitely help out with that."

Alec pressed a button on a small square device and a long thermoplastic strip emerged from it. He attached it to a ring around Lucy's neck. "It's a leash and collar," he explained. "For walking."

Britta did her weird half-smile. "I'll do it. I'll walk her."

She led Lucy toward the door, where Markus stood with crossed arms. "Oh, tell me you don't think she's the tiniest bit cute."

Markus shrugged. "Fine. I don't think she's the tiniest bit cute."

Britta punched Markus on the arm and laughed. "No way. Pet her, then tell me that."

Markus frowned. "I'm not touching that thing. Who knows what diseases it has?"

"She," said Britta. "It's a she, not an it. And *she's* way too cute to have a disease."

Britta pulled on her helmet, wrestled Lucy into an extra sunsuit, and marched past Markus into the street with the dog in her arms. "Come on, people, we haven't got all day."

Markus grunted and followed her out. He must have known he was way outnumbered on the dog issue.

Alec shrugged his shoulders at me, and grabbed his own helmet along with the enormous duffel bag. I smiled. He seemed like a good guy. He was certainly the first one I'd met that went out of his way to rescue an animal, let alone give it a cute name. Plus, he got huge bonus points for not shooting at me. James could learn a lot from him.

"Are you really as perfect as you seem?" I asked.

Alec's smile evaporated. "No one's perfect in this hell-hole of a world. It's just a matter of degrees of imperfection." He gestured for me to go ahead of him, and we exited onto the deserted street.

Once on board, the dog curled up at Britta's feet, causing her to gush more about how cute she was. The more Britta gushed, the more Markus scowled.

"Jealous of a dog, Markus?" I teased.

"Whatever. I guess I'll leave it to you then . . . you know, to explain the dog to Kale." He gunned the engine and we flew away from one desolate area toward another.

The mention of Kale's name was like a slap across the face. In an hour, I'd have to deal with James and Kale. I'd told Alec some basic stuff in our earlier messaging but that was before Markus overheard the whole "let's kill Tora" convo. I mentioned to Alec that Kale hadn't known we were coming for him, and wasn't happy about it.

"He's not happy with any of us," Britta added. "So don't be expecting a welcome wagon. Be on guard and don't trust them. Hopefully, we'll all get to Caelia and can go our separate ways." She eyed Markus. "Except for you . . . I'm thinking of hanging with you a while longer."

Markus laughed. "For a while, huh? Lucky me."

I didn't feel so lighthearted. Maybe there would be safety in numbers. I'd play the dumb and apologetic role, and hope I could get James alone to talk. Britta and Markus would back me up if things got bad.

"So what's your story, Alec?" Britta asked, looking over her shoulder at him. "Kinda fortunate that Tora found you, huh?"

Alec sighed. "No kidding. Seems we kept missing each other on the Net." He turned to smile at me. "I seriously don't know how to ever repay you, *mi ángel*."

I blushed. No one had ever called me their angel before.

Alec told Marcus and Britta the story about his friend and how he ended up alone in the pod city.

"Guess if you've gotta be stranded alone, it's better to be inside the pod city than out," Markus remarked. "I see why you hate the Consulate so much."

Alec's face darkened. "You have no idea."

I turned to Alec. "You got a gun?"

He patted beneath his shirt. "Yeah. Why?"

"You just might need to use it is why. That's all." I exhaled slowly and sank back in the seat.

Markus' com system crackled and beeped. He lobbed it underhand toward me. "Here, I'm sure you're the one they want to talk to."

Hesitating, I pressed my finger on the button. "We're heading back now—"

"No, don't come here." James spoke so quickly, it was hard to follow. "Leave us. I don't want you to—"

My heart pounded. What had happened? "James?"

Silence on the other end and then crackling.

"Tora, that you?"

"Yes . . . sir," I answered. My skin crawled at the sound of his voice. I'd hoped he'd had some sort of sun-related death while I was gone.

"Good, James got ahold of you. How far are you?"

"We should be there in thirty. We got the survivor. He's fine."

Alec pointed at Lucy, but I shook my head. Kale would put a laser blast through anything that couldn't pull its own weight, and he definitely wouldn't be giving it water.

"Great, glad he's okay. We've made it through half of the Consulate ship. Call when you get here."

I caught Britta's raised eyebrow. She knew as well as I did that Kale didn't care if the survivor was okay.

"Okay, Kale. We'll meet you there."

"That was interesting," said Alec.

"James was trying to warn us, I mean you," said Britta. "What should we do?"

"Going back there doesn't seem to be in anyone's best interest," Markus said.

Alec looked back and forth among us, as though we were a puzzle he couldn't figure out. He spoke slowly. "So why exactly are we going there?"

Britta scoffed. "Because Tora and James . . . well, it's complicated."

Heat flooded my face.

Markus looked back at me over his shoulder. "Are you sure it's worth it? If he cared enough to warn you, maybe we should listen to him and just head to Caelia."

Britta pulled her hand from Lucy's head and raised it in the air. "I second the motion."

"I want to see me some ocean," Alec added. "I owe you big-time, Tora, but I didn't plan to get rescued just to be killed by some *loco*."

I couldn't catch my breath and my heart pounded. I had

a much better chance of survival if I went along with the group, but I couldn't live with the version of myself that would leave. James knew he wouldn't survive long if we left, yet he'd been willing to sacrifice himself so that we'd be safe. That had to mean something.

If I didn't do the right thing, I'd have nothing. I wouldn't be my father's daughter. "I'm not leaving him. I can't do it."

"Look, sweetcakes, I get that you have mixed feelings for him, but I heard the dude say he would kill you. Britta's right that it's too big a risk—"

"Stop, Markus. It won't take long. Worst-case scenario, I die and you all go to Caelia without me."

Britta studied me while she continued to stroke Lucy. I fought the tears trying to overtake my eyes.

"Tora?" It was the softest I'd ever heard her speak.

"Yeah?" I stared straight ahead at the vast bloodred sky out the window.

"It's okay. We've got your back."

Alec leaned over and squeezed my hand. "Yeah, I definitely got your back."

I couldn't stop it this time. I cried.

Chapter EIGHTEEN

EVERYONE DOZED OFF ON THE FLIGHT BACK, TRYING TO GRAB a few minutes of rest before whatever came next. It felt like forever since I'd gotten a full night's sleep. I stretched as we approached our target. Only a few hours of daylight remained, and the sky glowed a brilliant reddish orange, making the entire landscape look like a raging inferno. The sun sure wasn't dying without a fight. It would be admirable if I wasn't made of such flammable material.

We landed fifty feet from the Consulate ship.

"You okay?" Alec asked.

I nodded, then reached to secure my satchel. A wet tongue greeted my hand, and I couldn't help but smile. "It's like she knows I'm upset."

Alec laughed. "It's crazy how much she knows."

I stood and stretched. T.O. in my bag and B.K. in my hand still didn't seem like enough if they started shooting right away.

I pushed the button on the com system and Kale picked up immediately. "Get your asses over here, we could use help."

Britta thought we should leave Lucy on Kale's ship for now, and I agreed. The fewer surprises for Kale, the better. If we waited until we were airborne to tell him, he'd have no choice. That's if Kale made it onto his ship at all. I hoped we could get away without him. Alec poured Lucy a bowl of water and put her in the hatch room until we got back. If we got back.

"Be a good girl," Alec told her.

I wasn't usually a betting kind of girl, but odds were the dog would outlast us all.

As I suited up for the brief trip, Alec caught my eye and winked like he knew everything would turn out okay. I wished I had his confidence. We stepped out into the sweltering air and ran for the Consulate ship. It had to be ten times the size of Kale's compact ship. Markus insisted on going in the main hatch first, in case Kale had planned an ambush. Britta, Alec, and I followed, and Alec stayed close to my side. No one was in the entryway when we got there.

I checked the oxygen reader on my Infinity, and called through the helmet coms. "The air reading looks okay, only a little lower than normal."

Alec removed his helmet and frowned at me. "That's

weird. Wasn't that gaping hole I just saw outside because of your shot?"

"Her slightly misguided shot," Britta added, but smiled.

"Why?" I asked.

"Because the air shouldn't be okay. It would mean someone sealed off the area around the damaged wing to keep the levels stable. And that would mean—"

"Survivors."

I jumped at Kale's voice and whipped my head around. He strode up to Alec and shook his hand. "I'm Kale. Nice to see they rescued someone with some brains."

Alec looked leery, but forced a smile. "Thanks, I'm Alec."

I sucked my breath in when James walked in behind him. This time he didn't avoid eye contact and his hazel eyes locked on mine—until Kale turned around. Then his eyes flicked to Kale. "James and I have scoped out the starboard side and haven't found anyone yet. Those bastards have to be here somewhere. Help us check out this side, then we just need to raid the med room, grab the spare parts, and go."

They'd been in the room with me for ten whole seconds and hadn't started shooting. Maybe Kale had changed his mind, or James had changed it for him. We moved down the hallway and an acrid smell of smoke filled the air. The hallways were black and burned, like fire had ripped through the ship. It must have been caused by the explosion when the ship crashed. I touched one of the walls, and came away with black ash covering my finger.

We came to a room with a huge window into the hallway, allowing us to view the suspended sleep pad and various medical equipment inside.

"Great. The med room. We'll stop here on the way back," Kale said.

We started moving past it when a laser came through the door, narrowly missing Britta. She dove and rolled on the floor, coming up on the other side of the door frame.

"Now!" Kale yelled and charged into the med room. James and Britta followed him, while I stood back with Alec and Markus. The room looked empty but there was a large white cabinet under the suspended sleep pad.

Kale's voice sounded calm and deadly. "We know you're back there, and there are six of us and only one of you."

It reminded me of the day when I was the one facing them, and I felt a little sorry for the guy. For about a minute. I had to do something to make Kale think I was with him one hundred percent, and my gun wasn't named B.K. for nothing. If it worked on boulders, taking out a med cabinet would be easy. With one shot from my gun, the cabinet vanished, bits of thermoplastic showering the air around the startled soldier. His eyes darted around the room, as if checking for other hiding spots. Not finding one, he dropped his gun and raised his hands in the air.

ZAP! ZAP! ZAP!

"What the—" I stopped midsentence as the soldier fell to the ground.

Kale and James continued firing until he stopped moving. Markus stood frozen, gun down at his side, and Alec's mouth hung open. They hadn't been kidding about the "no enemy survivors" thing. I tried to wrap my brain around the fact that James just shot an unarmed person. An unarmed person who had tried to surrender. James, who was supposed to save people with his medical skills.

Kale's head whipped around toward Britta. Her unfired weapon hadn't gone unnoticed. She held her head high, in clear defiance of yet another order. She'd refused to kill an unarmed soldier despite knowing Kale's rule. That earned her more points in my book. After what seemed like the most awkward silence ever, he turned away from her and nodded at James.

James walked over to me. "Hey, Tora."

My stupid heart skidded in my chest at the sound of his voice. Not like anyone would accuse his words of being romantic or anything, but still. He wouldn't have warned me to stay away if he didn't care about me a little. He reached down to touch my hand, and my knees almost buckled.

Until he jerked B.K. out of my hand. Before I could react, he passed it over to Kale. "Sorry about this."

"Nothing personal," Kale said, turning the gun over in his hand. "If there hadn't been survivors on board, I would've done this sooner." He raised an eyebrow. "James?"

James nodded. He pulled my hands in front of me. I

tried to pull away but in one quick movement he'd slapped handcuffs around my wrists. Old-school cuffs that required a real key rather than an electronic one. At least he'd cuffed my hands in front of me rather than behind my back. I'd spent all this time thinking James was really on my side, and it took him mere seconds to set me straight. The sun was turning out to be the least of my adversaries. At least it didn't discriminate with its destruction—I knew what to expect.

Markus held up a hand. "Whoa. No need for that, is there, captain? She just wanted to help a guy out."

"Yeah," said Alec. "It's my fault . . . sir. I begged her to come get me."

Kale stood taller. "Standard protocol. I just can't have her kidnapping my soldiers again." He stared at me. "I'm the only one with the key to those by the way." So that was why I didn't have the electronic cuffs. He was worried that someone might help me out. The thought gave me hope.

Britta's chest puffed up like she was about to give Kale a piece of her mind, but I shook my head slightly at her. Pissing Kale off wouldn't help me. Killing him would.

Kale sprang into commander mode. "Listen up. Britta and I will make sure the control room is clear. Markus, you and Alec move the parts and the last crate over to my ship. James, you stay here in the med room with this one." He nodded toward me. "Take whatever supplies you need, and we'll get out of here."

This one. I didn't even warrant use of my name. I'd

seen enough videos on my Infinity to know that the no-name character was the first to go. I was the red shirt.

"Can't Britta come with us?" Markus asked, his brow furrowed.

"Yeah, maybe we should all stay together," James added.

I gaped at James, not believing he'd questioned Kale's order. Especially not when he'd just disarmed and restrained me.

Kale shook his head. "I need backup, and you're the only one who knows what med stuff we need. I want to do this as quickly as possible. We'll see you in ten."

Britta ran to Markus and kissed him lightly on the lips. "Don't worry. See you soon." She glared at James with defiance. "Take good care of Tora. I mean it."

James met her eyes and gave a slight nod. She and Kale turned toward the front of the ship. They moved slowly with their weapons drawn.

Markus hesitated, then winked at me. He leaned in close to my ear. "Don't worry. We still have our guns and have no intention of handing them over. You'll be fine." He must have concluded that James was deceiving Kale. I wasn't so sure any longer.

Alec didn't look sure either. "You sure you'll be okay with this guy?"

James' jaw clenched. "I don't think anyone asked for your opinion."

Alec's chest puffed up and he took a step toward James.

Markus tugged his sleeve. "Easy there, big guy. She's fine." He pulled Alec out the door toward the main hatch.

That left me alone in the med room with James.

While being alone with James might have been my dream come true earlier, now it felt like a death sentence. At least I still had T.O. in my bag, and could probably grab it despite the handcuffs.

James packed some meds in a bag with his back turned toward me. I knew the com system was on but had to know why he was still going along with Kale. "James, I—"

ZAP! ZAP! ZAP!

I jumped at the sound of the gun, and my stomach dropped. It had come from somewhere inside the ship. James ran out of the room toward the sound. I followed as quickly as possible with my limited arm movement. He shouted at me to stay behind him, like there was a chance I could outrun him.

I had no idea what we were about to find, but my gut twisted inside. Either Kale was dead, which would be very good, or something very, very bad had happened.

Chapter NINETEEN

JAMES RACED TOWARD THE FRONT OF THE SHIP. I TRIED TO stay right behind him, which lasted all of five seconds before he shot ahead. Beyond the lingering scent of smoke, I smelled something else. It was nauseating but I couldn't place it, so I focused on my surroundings. A room up ahead had electronic metal panels along the walls on both sides. James leapt over something, not breaking stride. He went through the center of that room and disappeared through the next doorway. The smell grew stronger.

I panted as I ran, my hands useless in front of me. Panels with small holes for laser guns covered the walls of the room. It had to be weapons control. I pushed myself to run faster and catch up to James.

"What the hell is that smell?" I asked nobody in particular.

Then I tripped and fell on top of them.

Charred bodies lay on the floor underneath me. The smell was burned flesh. There were seven or eight bodies around me. I struggled to get up without the use of my hands but slipped on one of them. Skin slid off and stuck to my shoe as I tried to stand. Arms grabbed at me as I vomited onto the pile of corpses.

Alec and Markus stood on either side, helping to steady me. "Where'd you guys come from?" I asked, wiping my chin.

"Heard the gunshots from the ship and hauled ass . . . thought you were in trouble," Markus said.

Alec smiled. "You saved me. I thought it only right to return the favor."

Markus pulled a set of keys from his pocket. "Found them on Kale's ship. Thought they'd be mighty useful to you." He jingled the keys, and held up the smallest of the bunch. "This one looks about the right size."

A smile crossed my face. "Hurry."

"Patience, princess." Markus slipped the key in the lock and turned it. There was a soft click before the lock released. "Keep them on. Make it look like you're still locked up until we know what's going on."

I nodded and tried to ignore the stench invading my nostrils.

Markus surveyed the floor again. "Damn. That's nasty." He patted my back as I gagged again. "Pull yourself together, woman. What's ahead may not be much better."

I let them help me along until we'd gotten past the bodies. They'd died while attempting to kill us, but that didn't make me feel any better about it.

I gasped for breath as I jogged with my hands in front of me, and turned to Markus. "Can we please take Kale down now?"

"I think it's definitely time for a little mutiny," Markus agreed. "We outnumber him and can take his weapon. Easy."

I wasn't so sure about the easy part, but wanted to give it a try. Alec and Markus had their weapons in hand and I picked up the pace as we ran through the next doorway.

"You don't love guns much, do you, Markus?" I asked.

"Not really. Why?" he asked.

"Just a little funny for a gunrunner not to love guns, don't ya think?"

"Not really. How many people have worked jobs they didn't love because the money was good?" He stopped short as we reached the last room on the ship.

The control room.

Kale stood near the front of the room, facing the control panel. James bent over next to him, crouching over something on the floor. More dead bodies littered the room and the stench seeped out into the hallway. Bile roiled in my stomach but I forced it down. We stepped through the door. The bodies in here weren't as burned as the other ones. They must have succumbed to smoke inhalation.

"What's going on? Everyone okay?" Markus asked. He glanced at the bodies on the floor. "Where's Britta?"

No one answered. Behind Kale, I glimpsed Britta's skinny legs sprawled on the floor. James bent over her, holding her limp hand in his. He took it and rested it on her stomach, then stood to face us. His eyes flitted briefly to Alec, assessing him, before turning to Markus.

"She's gone. There's nothing I could do." James' face looked carved from stone. Expressionless.

"No!" Markus ran to Britta, and pushed James out of the way. Bright red blood seeped from the center of her chest. The shot had gone straight through her heart. The gun fell from Markus' hand as he sank to his knees in front of her body. "Dammit Britta, how could you die on me?"

Markus leaned down and touched his lips to hers. Though I'd thought about killing her myself little more than a day ago, something inside me broke. She'd been a scrapper, a survivor—like me. Markus had seemed happy when they were together. Now she was nothing. Gone.

Sadness and anger fought for control. Britta would tell me tears were for apocawusses. Sadness wouldn't help me now. Anger might.

"What happened?" I asked, staring hard at Kale. I knew what he thought about his enemies, and I wouldn't put much past him. Had he killed her?

"Bastard shot her," said Kale, pointing at one of the

bodies wearing a mask on the floor. "We thought they were all dead, but he got her when she came in the door. I took care of him, but not in time." He pinched the bridge of his nose with his fingers and shook his head as he looked down at her body. "It's my fault. I should have gone first."

Yeah, you should have. Maybe he thought some were alive and that Britta would make a good, disposable decoy. It was hard to know what to believe. The masked body on the floor did indeed have a gun in his hand and a chest full of fresh blast holes. Alec looked horrified and confused by the scene in front of him. James walked over to the Consulate soldier's body, stooping to take the gun.

"Can't hurt to have another gun," James said, then rose and brought the gun over to Kale. Great—now he had two guns.

Kale accepted the offering and turned to Markus. "I'm sorry. I know you had feelings for her."

James wore an odd expression on his face. "Nice work, captain," James said. "There don't seem to be any other survivors." I noticed him looking Alec up and down. Maybe he was a little jealous.

This was it. My heart raced and my palms started sweating. Stay calm, Tora. I'd have to take him out now, or we'd all be toast. Markus still crouched on the ground by Britta, seemingly confused and overwhelmed with grief. I didn't think he would be super-helpful in his current condition, so I flashed a look at Alec, hoping he'd catch on and jump in.

"Markus, I'm so sorry," I said. I walked over to him,

my hands in front of me as if the cuffs were still locked. In one quick motion, I pulled off the cuffs and scooped up Markus' gun that lay on the floor by his side.

I jerked it toward Kale. "Raise either of those guns and I'll shoot," I said, trying to control the shaking in my arm.

"Yeah, I'd listen to *una chica bonita* if I were you," Alec added. Out of my peripheral vision, I saw his gun also pointed at Kale. The fact that I was more terrified than I'd ever been in my life didn't stop me from registering the fact I'd just been called pretty.

Kale's face was grim. He turned to James, who looked away from him and walked over to me. James slowly raised his gun in Kale's direction. "I'm sorry, sir," he said.

Yes. I knew he cared about me. All that other crap had been an act.

"I'm sorry, sir," James repeated. He swiveled and pointed his gun at my head. "Sorry we have such pathetic traitors among us."

Alec started to swing his gun in James' direction, but James engaged his trigger panel. "Do it, and I'll shoot her," James said.

I shook with rage. How could James betray me like this? We were so close to getting away. The coldness in his voice as he threatened to shoot me felt like a knife going through me.

"No!" I yelled, too late.

Alec dropped his gun to the floor. "I can't let him shoot you. You saved me."

Markus finally snapped back into reality, and jumped to his feet. "What the hell?"

Alec hesitated a moment, which was all it took for Kale to raise his weapon and take back control. He fired a shot into the wall near Alec. Alec jumped, and Kale strode over to him. He retrieved Alec's gun from the floor.

Markus took a step toward me. James shook his head, his gun pressed to the side of my head. "Don't do it, man. Just stay there and no one will have to get hurt."

Kale pointed his gun at Alec. "What's it gonna be, soldier? The only reason I didn't kill you just now is I need you on Caelia. You look strong and able. But this is your one chance to convince me that you just made a terrible mistake. Can I trust you?"

Alec couldn't die. Somebody as decent as him had to live. He saved the last dog on the planet. Tears welled in my eyes. "Alec, you deserve to go to Caelia. Just do what Kale wants." *But I hope you kill these two burners when you get there.*

I couldn't decipher the look in Alec's eyes. "You can trust me, sir," he said finally. "But I am indebted to Tora for saving me."

James snorted. "Then do her a favor and get her to give up the gun."

Alec gazed into my eyes. "Give it to him, Tora. If you don't, the only way it can end is with you getting shot." He nodded toward Kale. "I don't understand everything going on here, but I'm sure it's just a big misunderstanding."

"Yeah, we can work this out. Give him the gun. Please," Markus added.

There didn't seem to be any hope of working anything out, but I was out of ideas. I sighed and held the gun in front of me. "Fine. Take it."

James reached out and only after he had my weapon in his hands did he remove his gun from my head. Asshole.

We were so screwed. Kale had all the guns, and it was impossible we could overpower James and Kale with our bare hands. We blew our only chance to turn the tables. If I used T.O., Alec and Markus would die too, and that wasn't an option I wanted to consider.

Kale's eyes flicked to Markus and Alec before he addressed me. "The only reason I'm not killing you right now is that I'm a more decent guy than you give me credit for."

No, the only reason you're not killing me right now is there are too many witnesses . . . unlike Britta. Kale was an observant guy. He'd already commented on Alec's intellect and strong build, and likely wanted to recruit him for his cause. He also knew Alec felt allegiance to me, since I'd saved the guy from certain death in the pod city. Maybe Kale realized that Alec wouldn't do squat for him if he killed me in front of them. I clenched my teeth to keep from responding.

James stood with his arms crossed, gun in hand. I wanted to charge at him and punch him, but I was more mad at myself for being such a sucker.

Kale handed the guns to James, keeping only his own. "See, no need for anyone to have guns anyway, now that we've killed all the bad guys."

"So no need for handcuffs again either, right? It's not like we can't handle a skinny unarmed girl on our own." I liked Alec more every time he spoke.

Kale's eyes flitted to me. "Fine. I'll leave the cuffs off you if you promise to behave." If he thought that would make Alec and Markus think well of him, he was delusional. He turned back toward the others. "Here's the deal. We'll take care of Britta's, um, body, and get out of here."

Kale didn't care about Britta's body, but knew that Markus did. I had to give it to him—he was smart.

I gritted my teeth. "Guess you don't need me, Kale. Alec and I can head back to the other ship and wait." I gestured for Alec to join me.

Alec tipped his finger to his brow, but his face was grim.

Once out of Kale's sight down the hall, I planned on somehow getting Markus, and booking it to Kale's ship to fly the hell out of there. James could go to hell.

"You're not going anywhere, Tora," Kale responded.

James assessed Kale, a questioning look on his face.

"Listen," said Kale. "Hear that? You can't go back now."

I'd been too distracted by dead bodies to hear the screaming of the winds. Night had come. The view out the control room window was one of near darkness, only a small reddish tinge lining the edge of the horizon. We were stuck here until the winds died down. We wouldn't make it fifty feet in these conditions. For some strange reason, I thought of Lucy and hoped she wasn't scared by the weather.

Instead of my grand escape plan, we all helped put Britta's body in a containment box, while I choked back tears. When she'd shoved me into one of those units, I'd wanted her to die a slow death. Now, just a short time later, I'd give anything to see that weird smile she had when staring at Markus or petting Lucy. Markus wanted to bring the box over to Kale's ship, then send her body out into space on the way to Caelia.

"She'd want to be free," Markus said, before putting his head in his hands.

Silence filled the room.

Kale and Markus carried the container with Britta's body to the hatch. As soon as the winds died, they'd transfer her over and we'd leave. In the meantime, we all trekked back to the med room through the enormous ship. There were so many hallways that branched off to different parts of the ship. Thoughts of Callie running and hiding popped into my head. My sister would have thought this was the most kick-ass place ever for a game of hide-and-seek, minus the dead people.

"Tora, can I see your Infinity a sec?" Kale asked like we were best buds. His face was anything but friendly.

Crap. I didn't want to do this. I reluctantly removed it from my wrist and handed it to him. "This was a gift from my dad." Like that would make a difference.

Kale fingered it a minute. "I've always wanted one of these. You mind if I play around with this a while?"

Yes, I mind, you freakin' burner. "Knock yourself out," I said, like it was a casual request. I knew I'd never see it again. My wrist already felt naked without it.

James strolled over to the table. His voice was mechanical, stiff. "Tora, help with these meds."

Screw you. "Sure."

"Toss the last few boxes in this bag, while I finish up with these others." He ordered it like I was his personal assistant or something. I wanted to clock him.

James glanced at Markus as he placed colored vials and boxes in the bag. "Any meds you want? There's some stuff here that'll help you feel better."

Great. He was sucking up to Markus, probably wanting to keep him on their side.

Markus slumped against the wall in a defeated posture. He wore the pain of a person who'd lost someone they really cared about. I knew that look.

"Great idea, James," Kale interjected. "Some of those will make you forget your own name. Might be good for you for a while."

Markus shook his head. "Nah. I don't want to forget."

"Suit yourself, soldier. James, make sure to stock up on those good pain meds I had before."

I wished he'd take them now, and go back to being belligerent but manageable. "Can I help with anything?" Alec asked softly, starting to walk toward me. His eyes looked pained, like he wanted to do something for me but didn't know what.

"No," James answered immediately.

"I think he was talking to me, not you," I answered.

James' jaw clenched, but he didn't say anything else. Alec went and stood awkwardly by Markus, his hands shoved deep into his pockets.

Alec had been nothing but nice. Anger surged in me. "Some friendly rescue team we are, Alec," I said, glaring at the back of James. "Sorry about that."

Kale peered at me while he strapped my Infinity to his wrist, as though daring me to say something about it. "Most rescue teams don't turn against their leader. You might have some trust issues, you know."

Markus laughed harshly and answered for me. "No shit. She doesn't trust any of us. That's no different than before."

Kale made a pathetic attempt at looking remorseful. "I'd hate to think you weren't with us on this, Tora, because that would make you . . . "

The enemy. He didn't need to finish his sentence. I shuddered involuntarily thinking again of the unarmed soldier. I'd already seen what this group did to their enemies.

"I know this girl better than anyone," said Markus. "I'll keep her in line." He looked like he could barely peel himself off the wall, let alone handle me.

"Okay. That should do it. Let's get out of here," said

James, tossing a final box into his bag. Once again, he avoided eye contact with me. You certainly wouldn't guess that he'd had his hands all over me not too long ago.

He walked by me and grabbed the supply bag from my hand. "Here, I've got this."

Kale grunted and walked out the door first. "Good work. Let's go."

James motioned for Markus, Alec, and me to go ahead, but managed to do it without looking directly at me. He'd told me to trust him but my gut told me I was a total dumb ass. I glanced behind me as I stepped into the hallway to join Markus and Kale. James did it so quickly, I might have imagined it. I thought I felt the touch of his fingers in my hair. Then they were gone.

Chapter TWENTY

KALE POUNDED HIS FIST INTO THE WALL OF THE CONSULATE ship. "Give me a goddamn break!"

The gale force winds of the night storms hadn't subsided yet. Pointing out that the storms sometimes lasted for several hours didn't seem like a helpful comment, so I kept my mouth shut.

Kale directed us to the kitchen where there were some energy packets and bottled water. This area had been spared from the worst of the fire. We sat at a table designed to hold five times as many men. Markus and Alec sat on either side of me at one end of the table, while James and Kale faced us. Fatigue permeated every bone in my body, but falling asleep was not an option. I couldn't protect myself if I slept.

No one seemed to feel much like talking. Guess they were as exhausted as I was. I felt James' eyes on me and though he looked away as soon as I met his stare, I caught the expression in them. Sadness. What did he have to be sad about? He betrayed me by choice. That look alone told me I wasn't going anywhere with them. No water-covered planet with trees in my future. Tears blurred my eyes, and I wiped them on my sleeve.

Kale cocked his head toward the ceiling. "I think it won't be long now. When the winds die, we'll run for it."

The winds wouldn't be the only thing dying if I couldn't figure a way out of this mess. I fingered my satchel. At least Kale hadn't taken that from me. I reached inside it and my fingers brushed the secret compartment containing T.O. I could kill Kale in a heartbeat with this. It was the killing of everyone else that kept me from pushing the button. Maybe I could bluff my way out with it though.

I felt the heat of Kale's stare. Should I try? If it didn't work, I would be completely out of options. Kale's stare intensified like he was about to take the bag. My hand knocked against Mom's diary, so I pulled it out like that's what I had been looking for. I flipped it open. "Don't mind me, I'm just going to read a dead woman's journal."

My fingers flew to the last few pages. If I was going to die soon, I should at least die knowing everything I could about my family. It wasn't like things could get any worse. I skimmed the journal entries prior to the last page. They were all by my mother. Tearstained entries about how much she missed the security of the pod cities and how bleak things were in the shelter. How painful it was to see her children living the life of prisoners belowground. How she'd have no reason to live if she lost us. How the pain meds were the only thing that numbed her depression and allowed her to function. I'd understood my mother was sad and hopeless about our situation, but I had no idea it was this bad.

Her pain-filled words became more rambling and hopeless as the pages went on. It was consistent with her increasing use of the drugs. The entries, which had at first been penned on a daily basis, grew sporadic. There were days, even weeks, between each one. Her last entry was a full two weeks before the date of her death.

I took a deep, shaky breath and turned to the last page. My father's handwriting stared back at me. There were no tear stains on his page, but then again, he was never a big advocate of feelings. *My heart bleeds today,* he began. A stabbing pain pierced my chest. He'd seemed so unemotional that day. He'd taken me aside after he'd found their bodies and tried to calm me. I was inconsolable and didn't understand his apparent lack of feelings. Reading the grief in his words made me aware of the depth of feelings he'd buried. Whether it was for his sake or mine, I'd never know. I kept reading.

My father wrote that my sister had been trying to sneak out on her own to go aboveground. I vaguely remembered that. She'd been so young when we lived in the pod city, where she was used to going outside without the need for sunsuits. Callie had craved the sun, loving its light, no matter the cost.

A memory of one of our last hide-and-seek games in the shelter flashed through my mind. *Come on, Tora, there's nowhere left to hide in here. It'll be more fun outside,* she'd begged. *If we go before the sun comes up, we won't have to wear the stupid suits.* Boy did she hate those sunsuits with a passion. *Are you crazy?* I'd asked her. I tried to explain about the night storms and freezing temperatures, but she'd sigh the same way I did whenever my father told me something I didn't want to hear.

I caught her once myself, climbing the ladder as fast as she could to get out. I gave her hell for it, and thought I'd ended her escape attempts for good. I took to locking the shelter door just in case, knowing it was difficult for her to unlock it herself. That way, I'd hear her if she tried to sneak out again.

I read more of my father's words. My mother had told him the door was locked, but that she still couldn't find my sister. He'd thought she seemed a little out of it from her latest "dose" and was merely disoriented more than usual. I'd apparently been napping at the time. My father wrote about his guilt over what happened in the next few minutes. He'd been so absorbed in his work that he mumbled "okay" when my mother told me she was going to look for her. It was a good ten minutes before the impact of her words hit him. I remembered the next part, when my father woke me to say he needed to go outside and look for them.

I froze at the next sentence. I read it again, blinked, and started over. I had to be reading it wrong. Since her death, I'd never allowed myself to cry over her for fear I'd never stop. I'd succeeded until now. Silent tears streamed down my face.

I know Tora didn't mean it; she didn't know that she'd gone outside again . . . that instead of locking her in, she'd locked her out.

I threw the journal onto the table.

"What's wrong? What is it?" Markus asked.

I killed my sister. The one person who meant more to me than anything. My little oasis in a sun-drenched world. My budding artist and lover of flowers. And I killed her.

"Nothing," I said. I closed my eyes to blot out the world, but a picture of what probably happened played on the inside of my eyelids. At the time my sister had still been alive and scratching at the door, my father had been working in the back room with his door shut, I'd been asleep with the music still playing through my ear pods, and my mother had likely been zoned out on pain meds. It was a miracle she'd noticed my sister was gone at all. But she had. And she'd gone up and found her youngest daughter dead on top of the shelter door she'd been frantically trying to open.

I knew without a doubt what she would have done next. Instead of screaming or yelling for help, Mom had simply gone out, taken off her sunsuit, and shut the door behind her. Her last shred of hope extinguished, she picked up my sister's body and placed her gently against the nearby rock. Then she'd curled up around my sister and waited.

Suicide by sun. My mother's will to live, which had been tenuous at best, evaporated completely at the sight of my little sister's body on the ground. Although I couldn't remember it, I must have wanted to sleep in peace so I'd locked the door to protect my sister while I slept. They died because of my selfish need for a nap.

I picked up the journal and put it back in my bag. Maybe I'd just let Kale kill me. Suicide by other. I was my mother's daughter after all. I put my head down on the table.

The room was quiet. Too quiet. No screeching winds in the background.

"It's about damn time," Kale said, stretching his legs. "I never thought that would end." He didn't even acknowledge my emotional state.

Kale and James stood and headed toward the hatch. Maybe they changed their minds about killing me here. Maybe once on Kale's ship, they planned to toss me out into space along with Britta's body. "You can keep her company," Kale would say as he pushed me through. He'd probably toss Lucy too, for good measure.

But Kale stopped halfway down the hallway. He slapped his hand against his forehead. "Damn, we left the bags back there. Markus, you run to the ship and get her started up. Show that new kid the ropes."

Markus looked at me. At least one person wasn't afraid to look in my eyes. "Nope. No offense, Kale, but you said we all needed to stick together."

"Yeah," said Alec. "I'm not going without *mi ángel*."

James didn't say a word but his hand clenched into a fist.

Kale's voice rose. "Soldier, I'm not chancing another night storm sneaking up on us again. Get over there and get us ready to go."

"It's okay. Go ahead, Markus. Just take Alec and go." I heard the dull, flat tone in my voice but I couldn't help it. Discovering that I'd killed my sister had put a crimp in my motivation to survive. Maybe this was karma. If I died, at least I had a chance of seeing her again—I could explain. I kept my eyes on the floor.

Markus jerked my arm and forced me to look up at him. "Seriously, I'm not leaving you. I feel responsible for this."

Kale snorted. "We don't have time for all this feelings crap. Get moving, soldiers."

Kale and James exchanged glances. They had guns and we didn't. Kale was probably weighing his options. If he forced Alec and Markus to do what he wanted now, he'd lose the "team" feeling he needed in order for Markus to help fly the ship and Alec to help with whatever his plan was on Caelia. He must have understood that playing for Team Kale didn't seem like such a winning proposition at the moment.

Markus squared his shoulders and stood straight. "We'll wait while you grab your bags. If you hurry, we'll make it."

James sighed. That one little expression changed some of my numbness to anger. What, was he annoyed that we were holding up the plan to kill me? Jackass.

James turned down the hallway. "It's fine, sir. I'll get the bags." He jogged back to retrieve the bags, and I watched his retreating form with a mix of bitterness and dejection.

Kale's eyes darted among the three of us, and his finger hovered over the trigger button of his gun which, while not aimed at anyone in particular, was noticeably still in his hand versus in his holster.

Alec glanced at Markus. Could we all just jump Kale and take him down before James got back? When Alec swallowed hard, and the muscles in Markus' arm clenched, I knew they were going to try.

James pounded back down the hall—two bags in one hand and gun in the other. Damn, he was fast. I admired him and loathed him all at once. Alec took a step back and Markus' posture relaxed. I'm glad they decided to wait, because who knows what would have happened when James rescued "his commander" again.

"Everyone ready?" Kale asked, trying for an easygoing, isn't-this-a-fun-adventure voice. To me, it sounded pretty much like his I'm-going-to-kill-you voice.

"Yes, sir," James said, hauling the bags farther up his shoulder.

I held the satchel close to my side. How long before they'd try to take it from me too?

The winds were calm, and once our helmets were on, Markus and Alec carried Britta's body to Kale's ship. We followed with the bags and spare parts. Only James and Kale carried the spare guns though.

The sad thing was, after reading the journal, I wasn't sure how I felt about the fact that Markus and Alec had bought me a little more time. If things had gone according to Kale's plan, I'd probably be dead already. I finally understood my mother's depression and pain, because if all those meds were in my bag instead of James' medical bag, I might have saved Kale the trouble of killing me.

I might have done it myself.

Chapter TWENTY-ONE

As the ship rose, a wave of sadness enveloped me as Earth grew smaller and smaller out the window. I'd dreamed of this moment every day for as long as I could remember. Now that it was happening, it didn't feel anything like I'd imagined when I was younger. Back in the pod city days, Mom and Callie would spin tales about the magical planet out there waiting for us. They would feed off each other and create a world filled with water and flowers—flowers of every variety and color. Their excitement was contagious, and I'd find myself thinking it might actually happen. I wished they had lived to see this.

We managed to get airborne before Lucy announced herself. Once the ship was up and on autopilot, Kale asked Markus to help move Britta into the hatch room. Markus decided they should release her body in deep space, and Kale was a tad overenthusiastic in his response. You'd think putting things out the hatch was his favorite pastime.

Markus had her body, tiny even when wrapped in a thermoplastic blanket, cradled in his arms. Kale moved to exit the control room, when Alec cleared his throat.

"Um, about the hatch room. See, there's a um—"

Alec's statement was interrupted by a muffled sound.

Kale drew his gun. "What's that noise?"

Alec jumped up. "No, I mean, it's just . . . my dog."

"A dog?" Kale asked, incredulously. "As in furry creature with a tail?"

"Yes, sir. That's what I mean. I'll show you."

The closer we got to the room, the louder the barking got. Kale pressed the panel on the door, but kept his gun in hand.

Lucy flew out and jumped all over Alec, licking his face and barking. Alec laughed and petted her. "Easy, girl, I said I'd be back." He reached into his pocket and fed her some sort of treat. Lucy scarfed it down without signs of chewing and then sniffed the air. She circled over to Markus and started to whimper, trying to nudge the lifeless form in his arms with her nose.

Markus looked like he was about to lose it, so I called Lucy over. "Come here, girl. It's okay."

Lucy moved backward hesitantly, but turned and came over to me. I pushed my hand into her soft fur, amazed at how comforting it was to touch her. She nuzzled my arm, and I smiled. My sister would have loved Lucy. My sister. I gulped, feelings of guilt breaking over me again.

"Does she drink a lot of water?" Kale asked, eyes narrowed.

Alec's eyes flashed with fear. "She does need some water . . . sir."

"Luckily, we have plenty of water on the ship, and it's everywhere in Caelia, right, Markus?" I asked.

Markus was laying Britta's body on the floor of the hatch room. He looked up with sad eyes. "Water?" His eyes focused on Lucy, and seemed to clear. "Oh, yeah. More than enough water for that mangy thing."

Kale grunted but didn't push the issue. For now.

• • •

The ceremony, if you could call it that, happened several hours later when we were in what felt like the center of the universe. Nothing but space around as far as you could see, and the dark vastness sent a chill through me. I was glad they kept the blanket around Britta when sending her out the hatch door. I had the irrational thought that she'd be cold without it. Kale wouldn't likely take the time to hand me a blanket when it was my turn. He'd just shove me out into the icy air.

We stood around Britta, and Kale tried to say a few words, but they sounded stilted and forced. *Because you killed her, you hypocrite.* Markus shook his head, too upset to say anything. I held his arm, a lump in my own throat. All

I could manage to say was, "I actually liked her in the end."

Alec shrugged. "I didn't know her long, but I trust my dog—and my dog loved her. If Lucy liked her, she had to have been good."

James went next, and I wanted to smack myself in the face when tears jumped into my eyes at his simple words. "Britta was Britta. You got what you saw with her—there wasn't a fake thing about her. I thought about what Britta would want people to say about her at a time like this." A wan smile appeared on his lips. "She'd want to end with this: Britta was no apocawuss."

A small half-smile escaped me. It's exactly what Britta would want said about her. The smile died quickly though. What would James say about me after I was killed? Assuming they even had a ceremony.

My hand gripped Markus' arm tighter and he patted me, probably thinking I was only reassuring him in his time of grief. Instead, I was grieving my own likely death. Guess I was selfish to the end.

After a few seconds of silence, Kale cleared his throat. "Why don't you do the honors, Markus?"

Markus moved Britta to the area near the hatch door behind a thick red line. Her hand fell out of the blanket as he set her down. He took her hand. "Good-bye, Britta. I'm sorry." His voice broke. "I wish I knew you longer is all."

He rearranged her hand under the blanket and stepped back to join us. Kale pushed an interior button in the room and a clear panel dropped down, enclosing the area behind the red line. A second later, the hatch door opened and Britta's body was sucked out into space. Her hand escaped the blanket once again, and it almost looked like she was waving to us as the door closed behind her.

"Good-bye," I whispered.

• • •

Markus downed the rest of his flask, which Kale had refilled several times using his own supply, and his eyes were red-rimmed and bloodshot. Everyone had been drinking, except for myself and James. Whatever happened next, I didn't want to die drunk. I'd even kept my suit on, minus the helmet, as if that could protect me from death. We sat in the small room used as a sort of combination dining hall and rec room.

Alec sat next to me, with Lucy settled between our chairs. We accidentally brushed hands a few times as we petted her, but there wasn't the electrical charge I felt when James had touched me.

"You know what I liked best about Britta?" Markus said out of nowhere. "You always knew where you stood with her."

James couldn't help but smile. "There's the understatement of the year."

Alec stroked Lucy's head. "I still can't believe how Lucy took to her so quickly. She can spot the good ones, that's for sure."

No wonder Lucy stayed far away from Kale.

"You really had a lot in common with her, Tora," Markus said, turning to me.

"Minus the whining. No one could complain the way she did," said James. His eyes locked with mine a second before he turned away.

I bit my tongue hard to keep from agreeing with James. "She told me you saved her life," I said to Kale. Maybe I could keep him talking long enough to figure out an escape plan.

Kale scoffed. "That's true. It's rough for survivors out there. Not everyone had the money your daddy did."

Bite me. I wanted to tell Kale all the good my dad did by protecting his family and keeping his lethal guns away from the world. That even though my mother hated leaving the comfort of a pod city and all it provided, and even though her depression grew worse every week after, my father knew it was best for us, for humanity, in the long run. But Kale wouldn't care about that.

Alec reached under the table and squeezed my hand. His touch was warm and comforting.

"Kale saved me too." James addressed me directly for the first time since we were in the med room. He ignored Alec entirely. At least he was finally answering my question. "I would have died if it wasn't for him.

"I first heard about him from Britta," James continued. "She said he attempted to stop some of the Consulate W.A.R. machine retrieval missions."

I couldn't help but notice Kale's clenched jaw

whenever Lucy wandered over to her bowl to slurp up some Caelia Pure. Like every drink she took was a form of stealing from him.

James' eyes flickered in my direction. "Anyway, one night the Consulate came to our pod and killed my family." This was the ultra brief version of the story he'd told me in the weapons room. "After my sister was killed, I closed my eyes and waited for it to be my turn. I heard more blasts but felt no pain."

Alec slammed his hand on the table. *"Asesinos!"*

James said that when he opened his eyes, the officials lay dead on the floor. Kale and Britta stood before him, armed to the hilt. The rumors were true. A rogue ex-Consulate operative was taking on the government. He'd learned that the Consulate was planning to sweep the pods outside the city walls to take what they wanted from the weakened survivors. It was exactly what Alec had described. Since Kale lived on the outside, he cared.

"That sucks." Markus was nothing if not succinct.

"Now you know our story," said Kale, no trace of emotion on his face. "See, I'm not such a bad guy after all."

Yeah, you've got a heart of gold. He'd probably done something to cause his fall from favor with the Consulate. If he'd remained inside the pod city, he wouldn't have given a damn what happened outside city walls. He likely would have helped them. His efforts were only in order to survive at all costs. Saving James and Britta allowed him to recruit more soldiers.

Soldiers that would owe him their lives.

"So you never intended to give them the guns then?" I asked Kale.

He smirked, clearly feeling the effects of Markus' drink. "No, ma'am. I intended to collect payment and then use the guns to take those burners out. Finding out that only you could fire them put a small wrench in the plan, but I'm used to overcoming obstacles." He made eye contact with James.

I might as well have a neon light across my head flashing the word *obstacle*. I tried to catch Markus' eyes, but they were off in a distant, painful place. He had to pick now to turn into a human being with feelings? It would have helped me more if he'd stayed an asshole—and sober—just a bit longer. I didn't have a gun or my Infinity. I rubbed the empty spot on my wrist where the Infinity used to be. I needed help. Even Alec seemed drunk and barely able to keep his eyes open.

Kale banged his hand on the table in front of Markus. "Soldier, you're not lookin' so good. Maybe you should get yourself some shut-eye."

Markus rose unsteadily to his feet. I attempted to help him, but he shook me off. "I'm f-f-fine. I got it. Just need some time to sleep off this nightmare." He made an attempt to look at me through heavy-lidded eyes. "Get me if you need me. I'm"—he tripped a little—"here for you." Markus stumbled out of the room and down the hall.

Alec's head tipped forward and his chin touched his

chest. He seemed to be mumbling but lifted his head with great effort. "I'm beat too. Tora, you can crash with us." Except his words slurred together and sounded more like torayoucancrashwithus.

My heart sank. I wanted to kick myself because it had taken me so long to realize that they were drugged. Kale must have added something special to that last batch from the flask. I hadn't noticed that he'd stopped drinking.

"Wait, Alec," I called, playing along like he was just drunk. I brought Lucy to him. "Here, take Lucy with you. She needs some sleep too." I ran my hand through her fur one last time. I'd miss the dog most of all. I stood and whispered in Alec's ear. "Lock your door." Though I was hatch bound, at least maybe Lucy would be safe for another day.

Alec attempted to look at me, but his eyes remained cloudy and unfocused. "Okay."

Lucy turned and licked my hand before trotting off behind Alec's staggering body. Alec and Markus would sleep through Armageddon tonight. No screams, cries, or even explosions would permeate their stupor. They would wake tomorrow, likely with a headache from hell, and wonder what happened.

I could already hear Kale's explanation for my absence: *Tora was more broken up about what was in that journal than we thought. Remember how upset she got? She must have thrown herself out the hatch.* Then Kale would read aloud from the journal and nod sympathetically. *Oh, see here, she killed her* sister and her mother committed suicide. *No wonder she killed herself.* My stomach lurched, because it was actually believable. I'd thought of overdosing too—it was the first time I'd thought of the meds as a means of suicide rather than simply a practical way to avoid burning to death.

Kale must have been thinking along the same lines. "So, it's just the three of us now." He stood, clearly not as drunk as he'd seemed a few minutes ago. "I'd like to have a look at that satchel of yours, Tora."

Here we go. My eyes darted to James. It would be so easy. Hand over the bag and let them shoot me. It would be over within minutes, and I wouldn't have to deal with these burners or this crap world ever again. But my hand tightened on the bag. My dad's voice filtered through my head. *What's it gonna be, Tora—die or die trying?* His voice told me that it wasn't my fault they died, that I had a responsibility to live for all of them.

I took a small step away from Kale and James. "No." It wasn't a great option, because it's not like I had a lot of places to go. My only choice would be to go back deeper into the ship.

James stood and folded his arms. "Maybe you misunderstood the commander. It wasn't a request, it was an order."

The coldness in his voice shook my resolve.

Remember who you are. There was Dad's voice again, reminding me that I was the only one who could stop the guns from being used for mass destruction. I thought of

Markus and Alec, and realized I still had people in this world I could trust.

I took another step backward, trying to control the shaking in my legs. "My answer is still the same. Hell, no."

"Last chance." James spoke in a low, hostile voice. He pulled his weapon from his waistband and trained his gun on me. Seriously? The boy who had touched my ribs like they were the most fragile thing on Earth must have been a figment of my imagination. It's a shame I wouldn't live long enough to win the worst-judge-of-character award.

My first instinct was to cry—the second one was to run. I went with the second and took off in a zigzag pattern down the hall.

"I'll get her," James yelled and lasers bounced off the walls around me.

I tore down the ship's corridors, looking for a place to hide. Kale's ship was nowhere near as large as the Consulate ship. This was officially the worst game of hide-and-seek I'd ever played.

I thought of my family as I leapt through a doorway and ran faster than I had in my life. It was amazing how athletic I became when death was on the line. Still, I was no match for James. Footsteps pounded behind me, closing in. If I continued going straight, I'd end up at the end of the ship and I'd be trapped. I veered down a smaller hallway to my left and looked to my right.

Several doors were open. I picked one in the middle and jumped inside. I wedged myself between the open door and the wall, hoping that if he turned on the light, he'd think the room was empty. My throat and chest burned from the exertion. I tried to calm myself and not dwell on the fact that the person chasing me was James. Footsteps raced by at a distance and I figured he'd taken a different hallway.

I sagged against the wall. If only it were my sister looking for me, and not someone who made my stomach flutter despite the fact that he wanted me dead. Someone who didn't care about anyone other than himself.

The footsteps circled back, slower now, more deliberate. They grew louder as they neared my hiding spot. Trying not to make noise, I slid my hand inside the satchel, unzipped the inner compartment, and gripped T.O. I might not be able to save the new planet from the Consulate, but there was still a chance I could keep my father's guns out of the equation. No wonder he regretted creating something that only brought destruction. I couldn't remember anyone describing what a great time they had on the receiving end of a gun.

The footsteps stopped in the hallway outside the door. I couldn't tell if the rapid breathing I heard was mine or his, as I pulled T.O. out of the bag. The light turned on. My heart skidded in my chest as James stepped through and swung the door shut behind him. An involuntary gasp caused him to swivel around and face me. The twinge of relief I felt at his being alone was erased when he raised my own gun at me. I sucked in my breath. He held B.K. in his hands like he owned it.

"Move out here in the center of the room."

I moved but held T.O. in front of me like a sword.

"Is your com system on, James?" At least if it was on, I'd understand a little better why he was doing this.

"No, I told Kale I would do the job but that you deserved a private death. Consider this a favor, because he wanted to kill you himself, and he'd have done it using the hatch."

Private death? Was I supposed to be grateful that it was an exclusive event? Next he'd tell me about how this was part of his master plan. I stood and took a step toward him. "James—"

"Step back. Now." He raised B.K. higher.

I couldn't believe this was happening. "If Kale doesn't need me alive, he must know that you can fire the weapons too. You told him. I'm an unnecessary complication—just like Britta was."

"Pretty much, except I didn't tell him. He figured it out that day—said we both looked scared out of our minds." James looked torn, but kept checking the door. As if he thought if he stayed too long, Kale would come bursting through it.

"You're admitting he killed Britta?"

He confirmed what I'd only guessed. "I knew as soon as I touched the Consulate guy's gun that it hadn't been fired recently. Also, that soldier had been dead a while. There was no blood."

No blood. Of course. I'd noticed the blast holes in the

soldier's chest when I'd run into the room, but there wasn't any blood gushing from his chest. He'd died soon after the ship crashed.

My heart sank. James knew all this about Kale, yet still refused to go against his commanding officer. "Why are you doing this? What about that time in my room?" I could barely squeak the words out, afraid of the response.

He hesitated, "It's not that simple. I told you Kale is part of something bigger. I need him to find—"

"So you're in this for your own gain." Anger rose red-hot inside. "Why should I be surprised? It's what everyone else does around here. Well, go ahead. Take me out, you burner." *Come on, James, this is the time for you to tell me how this is all an act.*

James didn't respond. At least he had the decency to look ashamed. His jaw clenched and he placed his finger on the trigger panel. I heard the familiar hum as B.K. powered up. Even though it was my gun, it would destroy me the same way it did those boulders or that stack of books. T.O. was the only weapon my father felt the need to design special, since it was a bomb and all. T.O. couldn't hurt anything at my vibration, but my gun? My gun had no freakin' loyalty. Yet I still couldn't make myself pull T.O.'s trigger.

He aimed B.K. at me, then pulled another gun with his left hand, which he aimed at the center of my chest. I guess he wanted to make sure I was really, really dead. "I'm sorry, Tora. This isn't what you think."

An alarm sounded overhead and red lights seemed to flash everywhere at once.

James looked around, confused. He flicked on his com system. "What the—"

"James—get back to the control room, pronto." Kale's voice sounded through the device.

"What is it, sir?" he asked, lowering both guns.

I hadn't realized I'd been holding my breath until the guns weren't pointed at me anymore. I exhaled in a rush and dropped T.O. back in my bag.

"Consulate ships," Kale said. "Three of them are on our tail."

While Consulate ships chasing us was not any better than, say, a gun pointed at my heart, or a well-oiled hatch door, I sighed in relief anyway.

The relief lasted about five seconds, at which point I was flung by an unseen force into the wall next to me. My face smashed into the metal, and James fell next to me. He managed to secure the smaller gun in his waistband, but B.K. fell from his hand. I tried to bend down and reach for it, but couldn't peel myself off the wall.

I could barely speak, and the words felt as though they were being torn from my throat. "What's going on?" I asked James.

James struggled to speak as well, yet had somehow managed to get his grip back on B.K. "Hyperdrive."

He took another breath and looked me straight in the eyes. "We're running from them."

Chapter TWENTY-TWO

THE HYPERDRIVE LASTED ABOUT ANOTHER TEN SECONDS, though it felt like an eternity. I crashed to the floor without warning. "That's crazy," I said, more to myself than James.

"Well, normally, you're supposed to be buckled in during hyperdrive—"

I stared at James in disbelief. "I'm not talking about that. It's crazy to run from the Consulate. Aren't their ships faster than Kale's?" I noticed he wasn't pointing B.K. at me. Maybe I could wrestle it from him.

"Yeah, their normal speed is faster but they've been upgraded, so their hyperdrive was replaced with warp drive."

"Yeah . . . and?" I asked. Now it was his turn to look at me like I was a star short of a constellation.

James sighed. "Their regular speed is faster than our regular speed, but it's not as fast as our hyperdrive. Their only other drive is warp drive, which is way faster than our hyperdrive, just not as controllable. They'd overshoot us by light-years. This only buys us a little bit of time though. They'll find us."

James' com system crackled. "You coming, soldier?"

"Yes, sir . . . Tora's with me." James kept B.K. pointed at the floor rather than at me.

"We'll deal with that later. Bigger things on our plate right now," came the response. "Get up here."

I glared at James. "Shouldn't we tell Markus and Alec what's happening?"

James looked matter-of-fact. "No use. They won't be awake for a while yet."

I wanted to run, but he gripped my upper arm with his hand and propelled me out the door toward the control room. He yanked me down the hall. "So James, what's so important that you're willing to kill for it?"

He gripped my arm even tighter. We neared the control room. He spoke through clenched teeth. "I'll explain after."

I laughed harshly. "What? You mean after you kill me, you'll have a chat with my dead body. Thanks so much."

He pushed me into the control room where Kale punched various buttons with intensity. He studied some sort of graph by the controls and spoke. "We only have a little time before they track us again. There's a small planet just ahead that seems to have a strange energy field around it. It's messing up my readings. If we hide out there, it might just create enough interference that the Consulate ships won't be able to track us. We can wait until they pass by, and hyperdrive back to a path to Caelia."

As far as plans go, that didn't sound like a great one.

James frowned. "You mean land there? If the planet's energy messes up our systems way out here, who knows what it will do to our ship when we pass through its atmosphere. It could destroy us."

I gulped. *Yeah, what he said.*

Kale spun around. "You got a better plan, soldier? We can't hyperdrive again until the system recharges—they could catch us by then." Kale scratched his head. "I'm still trying to figure out how they found us in the first place. It's like they knew where we were."

James paused a moment. "I have no idea, sir. You're right. Landing there is our best shot."

Great. Being pulled apart by strange magnetic forces seemed way worse than a shot through the heart. On the positive side, with every new potential method of death presented to me, the more sure I was that I wanted to live.

Kale punched some coordinates into a virtual keyboard that appeared in front of him. The ship dove lower toward the distant planet. James pointed me toward a seat and he sat in the one next to it. When I pressed a button on the chair, mechanical restraints enclosed me in a tight embrace. The boy I'd thought was my dream guy sat within a foot of me, yet the only thing touching me protectively was a thermoplastic harness. Story of my life.

"Hang on," Kale called before pushing his own restraint button.

The descent became faster and steeper, and I wondered if I'd actually feel anything at all if the ship suddenly ripped apart. The satchel pressed into my side as we hurtled through space. A roar ripped through my ears when the ship entered the planet's atmosphere, and the entire ship began vibrating. My heart had pretty much lodged itself in my throat, and I gripped the arms of my chair with white knuckles. The vibrating turned to violent shaking—it reminded me strangely of my mother's withdrawals when she'd tried to quit the pain meds. Something popped and a piece of plastic flew through the air, inches from my head.

"Not a big deal," Kale yelled above the noise.

A second later, something else popped, and a hissing sound added to the grating sound of the shaking ship.

"That was a big fuckin' deal!" Kale screamed. The shaking came to an abrupt halt, though the hissing remained. Kale furiously worked on the control panel, sweat breaking out on his brow. If he was flustered, it couldn't be good.

"What is it, sir?" James asked. Even he was pale.

"The pressure for the fuel system of the landing rockets. Without it . . . well . . . " He didn't finish his thought, and continued pushing buttons in random succession. I guessed he was trying to manually override the system.

Something must have worked, because the hissing stopped and a new humming sound took its place.

I opened my mouth to ask about it but we hit the ground first. The ship screeched and lurched in protest against the planet's surface. If not for the protective restraints, I likely would have been thrown right through the windshield. It made me wonder about Alec and Markus, and I hoped Lucy was okay. The ship groaned as it finally came to a stop.

Kale pushed a button and his restraints retracted. "Not bad. The thrusters weren't able to fully engage in time, but any landing you can walk away from is a good one."

The scene in front of us was strange. The surface of the planet seemed to shift and move around us. Mountainous hills arose on either side of the ship, then shrank and grew again into a different formation. The ship rumbled as it crested on a mound that formed beneath us.

I pushed the button on my own harness. "I want to check on the others," I announced. Right before I find a way outta here.

Kale looked at James. "Take her, but come right back."

I sprinted down the hall, James following after me. "Wait up," he yelled. He'd tucked B.K. into his waistband too, which gave me a small, though temporary, sense of relief.

The ship lurched again as the ground beneath us changed shape, and I grasped the wall to steady myself. Lucy's pitiful whimpering sounded from inside the room, and she scratched desperately against the door.

"It's locked from the inside," James said, waving his hand over the panel to no avail.

At least Alec had listened to my warning. "Is there an override system?" I asked.

James called up to Kale, who must have done something, because the door opened a second later. So much for my plan to keep Lucy safe—Kale could open whatever door he wanted at any time. Lucy bounded out the door and into my arms. "You're okay, girl. It's okay. Just a little rough landing is all."

I stepped into the room and almost stepped on Alec. Markus lay on the floor a few feet away. James leaned down to check each of them. "Their breathing and heart rates are fine. They must have rolled out of the chambers during the descent."

My eyes widened. "You're telling me they slept through that. What the hell did you give them anyway?"

James didn't answer. Lucy padded over to Alec and tried to nose her way into his pocket for treats. James absently put his hand on her back and petted her a second before realizing what he was doing. He jerked his hand back and stood up. "She's hungry. You can bring her food and water, but keep her back here, away from . . ." He paused, and looked at Markus and Alec. "Let's go. They'll be fine."

I snorted. "Yeah, until you give them their next dose."

James ignored me. His footsteps echoed behind me as I headed toward the kitchen to find something for Lucy to eat. Guess I wouldn't be going anywhere without his company. I had to figure something out fast. As I neared the kitchen door, I scanned the hallway ahead. The entry hatch to the ship was at the end of it. Everyone except me had removed their suits, which hung by the main hatch door. Since my suit was still on, all I needed was one of the helmets tossed nearby on the floor.

Hide-and-seek on a ship of this size would only last so long, but I might have a chance on the planet. If Kale was right that the Consulate would eventually find us, maybe they would come sooner rather than later. The Consulate rescuing me was a long shot, but it wasn't like I had an abundance of options at the moment.

Though the surface seemed way unstable, if it could hold the weight of the ship, it would hold me. Plus, the multitude of hills would provide great hiding spots. James was fast, but he'd need to put on his whole suit. If I could just make it through the door. My muscles tensed. I had to try.

The ground moved again and the ship settled back hard against the surface. I stumbled, crashing into James, who fell against the wall. My face was so close to his I could feel his breath, and his arms caught me around the waist. My skin tingled at his touch and goose bumps broke out along my arms. His lips came closer to mine, and for one second, I was positive he was going to kiss me.

A part of me wanted to believe he'd finally come to his senses, and maybe now we could get the hell out of here. The other part of me knew better.

Kale's voice tore from the com system. "James, it's time to carry out the final orders, soldier."

James sighed and dropped my hand. "Yes, sir." Since his com system was on, I guessed I wasn't getting a private death this time around. He pulled out both guns from his pants and powered up B.K. I remembered what he said about being a great shot, that he could kill me with one shot from a long distance. At present, he was less than a foot away and had not one, but two guns. I was so dead.

"Seriously? Why two guns if you're such a great shot?" I asked, right as a mountain formed underneath us, and pushed the ship upward at a strange angle. We tilted sideways, teetering in the air.

James fell sideways, and I stumbled as fast as I could toward the main hatch. My pulse raced and I propelled my legs faster, hoping the ship would stay unbalanced for a minute longer. My feet kept slipping on the angled floor, so I used my hands to help navigate toward my goal.

"Stop!" he yelled after me. "It's dangerous out there."

Was he serious? "Yeah—you shooting me is so much safer!" I yelled.

"Shoot her already," I heard Kale shout through the com.

I scrambled for my helmet, and pushed the hatch door button. My heart hammered as I tried to attach the helmet to the suit, but my hands shook so badly that it took several attempts.

The hatch opened and I ran outside, only to realize

that the ship rested on the peak of a very tall mountain. My feet slid out from under me, and I landed on my butt and started sliding down the steep side. I picked up speed, wishing I had more padding in my rear as I hit every bump on the way down. Tons of smaller hills dotted the area around me. At the rate I was going, I'd be nothing more than a splat on the ground when I hit bottom. The sound of yelling in my helmet com startled me, and I looked up to see James coming out the hatch door, gun in hand. Damn, he was fast.

The ground came faster and faster, and I had seconds until impact. I shut my eyes and braced myself. Rapid shifting occurred under me, and the ground leveled. The ship slammed down behind me as the mountain disappeared as quickly as it had come. I opened my eyes and turned around. The ship was several hundred feet away, but James was halfway to me and closing in fast. I jerked myself to my feet, ignoring the throbbing pain, and ran toward a cluster of hills that had newly formed. There were about twelve of them—I just had to hide long enough to figure out a new plan.

My breathing came in ragged bursts. I ran into the hills and kept going until I found a small enclosure in one of the farthest ones. I sank to my knees and tried to catch my breath. I pulled T.O. out of my satchel, though I wasn't sure what good it would do. Even if the bomb destroyed Kale and his ship, it would kill the others too, except maybe James, and I'd be stuck on a bizarre planet. I was totally screwed.

"Just tell me where you are, Tora," James' voice pleaded through my helmet.

I stood and leaned against the alcove in the hill. I didn't want to sound as weak and tired as I felt. "You'll never find me," I said with false confidence.

Guess I spoke too soon, because the planet shifted again and all of the hills disappeared at once. James stood several hundred feet away. There was nothing between us. His voice was calm. "I have to do this."

I heard Kale's voice through James' com system. "I have a visual on you, James. Good work. Finish her and get back to the ship."

A roar in the sky made me look up. The Consulate had found us. One ship was about to touch down, and two other small dots in the distance had to be the other ships.

I flicked the switch on The Obliterator and raised an eyebrow at James. "Does this change anything?" My finger hovered over the trigger panel.

He shook his head, and trained both guns on me. A shot tore into me and pain flooded my senses. Everything around me turned blurry and seemed to happen in slow motion.

The roar of the Consulate ship grew louder as it landed. What seemed like fifty soldiers poured out of the ship, weapons drawn. Behind James, I saw Kale's ship lift in the air and gun for the horizon. I opened my mouth to speak but the pain was too great, so I pointed instead—maybe Kale deserting him would change his mind about shooting again.

James gazed skyward as Kale's ship departed. He lowered his gun and ran toward me, "Tora! Don't move. I'm coming—"

That's when the soldiers took aim en masse at James. A shot ripped into his leg and another went through his arm. My heart lurched despite the fact that he'd just shot me. I couldn't watch him die. Plus, if they didn't realize who I was, they'd turn on me next. I gripped T.O. with my last remaining strength.

God help us all. I pushed the button.

Chapter TWENTY-THREE

LAUGHTER FILTERED THROUGH THE MIST AROUND ME. GIRLISH laughter. I flew through the air, attempting to locate the source of the sound. The wind caressed my hair, blowing it in tangles around my face. I wore no sunsuit, and the sun warmed my skin, yet didn't cook it. I broke through the foggy substance and followed the childlike giggles. The sky was a brilliant blue, dotted with a thick substance I knew were clouds, even though there had been no clouds for centuries. The sun was warm yellow in color, bearing no resemblance to the red inferno of Earth. I inhaled the scent of fresh clean air—and flowers. Wildflowers. Some-how I knew what everything was without being told.

"Callie!" I called. Her name felt like sugar in my mouth.

I tried to fly faster. Leaves and flowers floated down on me as I soared through the sky.

"Come and find me," Callie called back, her giggles echoing in front of me, behind me, everywhere.

"It's not funny, Callie. Come out. I want to see you."

The scent of wildflowers grew stronger and a single calla lily floated into my hand. I grasped the flower and inhaled deeply. It was how I'd imagined it would smell. Soft and sweet like my sister, which was why I nicknamed her after a flower. *I'm going to find you, Calla lily*, I'd call after her. She loved it when I called her by that name.

"I picked it for you. Do you like it?" she asked. Callie floated before me, dressed in her favorite floral shirt. She still didn't look a day over seven years old. This time when I reached out for her, my fingers didn't touch just air. The material of her shirt felt strange in my hand. Not quite solid, but still tangible.

"It's really you?" I asked. She nodded and I flung my arms around her to hug her. Her body felt more like a rippling energy wave than human. She blinked in and out of physical form. "Callie, I'm so sorry. I shouldn't have locked the door that day. It's all my fault." Tears cascaded down my face and dripped onto her blond ponytail. I tried to smooth her hair with my hand, but couldn't seem to touch her actual hair.

She looked up at me with shimmery eyes. "It wasn't your fault. All you ever did was try to keep me safe. I shouldn't have gone out there—you warned me."

How could she forgive me so easily? "Callie, where's Mom?"

Callie smiled. "She's around. She's much happier now. She loves you so much and is sorry for causing you pain."

This caused a fresh wave of tears. My throat felt like a lump of dirt had wedged itself inside. I'd never let my sister out of my sight again. "I'm so glad we're together. I'll make it up to you, I promise."

Callie cocked her head to one side, as if she was listening to something that I couldn't hear. She turned around to look behind her. All I saw was the vast expanse of blue sky. Callie frowned when she turned back around. Her voice sounded farther away, even though she remained right in front of me. "You can't stay, Tora. You're still needed down there."

"No way. I finally found you. I'm not going to leave you." But Callie began to fade away.

She flew to me and kissed my cheek, a buzz of warm energy against my skin. Then she danced out of reach, skimming over a cloud as she moved farther away from me. "Don't worry, we'll see each other again before you know it."

"Don't go!" I screamed. I fought as my body propelled itself down toward the planet below. Air currents ripped through me as I descended.

"No!" I yelled. Nobody listened.

I heard Callie's faint voice despite the distance. "I love

you, Tora," she called as I went back through the clouds. My view was obscured by the fine, white vapor.

"I love you too, Callie," I called back. Her small, tinkling laugh answered me, spreading warmth through my chest. Though my body felt more solid and heavier with each second, a great weight lifted from my shoulders.

"Ms. Reynolds." It wasn't Callie's voice. No clouds, no flowers, no leaves surrounded me. No nothing, except blackness.

"Ms. Reynolds." The voice grew more insistent.

My eyes opened a crack, allowing a sliver of light to penetrate. I squinted and squeezed them shut again. My throat burned. God, I craved water.

A hand touched my arm and shook it. A firm shake, definitely not gentle. "We need you to wake up now."

"And I need water," I croaked, keeping my eyes shut tight. When a bottle was pressed into my hands, I forced myself to open them. Damn, the light was bright in here. Maybe I was dead; maybe I'd died on that strange planet. Other hands propped me up into a sitting position.

Everything was blurry, yet I managed to bring the bottle to my lips with a little assistance from the various other hands in the room. I sipped the water. It was cold. My eyes opened wider. The water was cold. This was what cold was. Where the hell was I if not dead, because who had cold water?

A man in wire-rimmed glasses and a shiny silver coat approached me. "Ms. Reynolds, it appears you've been shot."

"No shit. Tell me something I don't know."

A murmur ran through the room. How many people were in here anyway? Trying to look around made me dizzy and my vision blurred further. "Sshhh, take it easy. You've been through a lot." More hands leaned me back against the pillow. I took the bottle with me, not caring that I was sloshing water down the front of my gown every time I took a sip. If I was in a gown, this had to be some sort of medical facility.

I gulped the rest of the water, then waited for my vision to clear. The room was stark white, which only made the light seem brighter. I waved my empty bottle in the air, and someone brought me a refill.

"How'd I get here?" I asked, looking around. There were eight or nine figures in the room, and they all wore long coats. Only the man in wire-rimmed glasses had a shiny silver coat though. He must have been the one in charge, because he addressed my question.

He scoffed. "You mean before or after your little bomb destroyed two of our ships? We had to stop chasing Commander Stark to come back and retrieve you. He got away and many of our men's lives were lost thanks to you."

Kale's last name was Stark? Though I wasn't happy he got away, it meant Alec, Markus, and Lucy were safe—for now at least. I attempted to sneer at the wire-rimmed man, but choked on my water. It dribbled down my chin. "You know that eyeglasses went out of style like two hundred years ago, right?"

One of the women in the room, dressed in a shiny green coat, smiled. "He thinks it lends an air of authority." She shut up after Mr. Wire-Rims shot her a nasty look. I wondered what one had to do to earn a shiny coat. I'd like mine in lavender.

Wait. Clothing reminded me of my satchel. I swiveled to check around me. "Where's my bag?"

The man pushed his glasses up higher on his nose. Did no one else realize how crazy it was to wear glasses as an accessory? "Your bag is fine . . . it was on your body when you triggered the bomb. Now, about you. We found you after receiving the distress call on the com system," he said smoothly.

"What distress call?" I asked, genuinely confused.

The man came closer. I felt his touch even though he wasn't near enough to reach, and shivered. "The young man was worried that Tora Reynolds—only survivor of the great Dr. Micah Reynolds—was going to be ambushed."

Young man? Had Markus found a way to contact the Consulate? If not, who the hell were these people?

"I'm sorry. I've been rude," the man said, peering over the glasses now. I had a strange urge to rip them off his face and smash them. "I'm Dr. Sorokin." He extended his hand to me. I reluctantly shook it, his hand cold and clammy against mine. I took it back, rubbing it against my gown.

"You were lucky. The shot only hit your shoulder." His smile stretched awkwardly across his face.

"Huh? Only one shot?" I distinctly recalled there being

two guns, one of which was B.K. One shot from B.K. would have blown me apart. Maybe I was dead and hell was a place with people in eyeglasses and shiny coats.

"Yes, just the one," he said, eyeing me strangely. "We certainly wouldn't know otherwise, being that your bomb blew everything to bits."

I sat up again. That didn't make any sense. James said himself that he was a perfect shot. Missing any vital organs was one thing. Missing me entirely using one of the deadliest weapons in existence was highly unlikely. All I knew was that if I had it to do all over again, I would have killed them all the second I had the chance. I'd never let myself be vulnerable again.

"Ms. Reynolds, you know that you're quite famous due to your father. You got lucky—we were already on the way to see what the holdup was regarding a business matter. Your way of thanking us was not very hospitable." His eyes narrowed at me. "The only reason we didn't kill you for your treason is that you are of some value to the Consulate due to your . . . weapons abilities. The caller said that you'd be able to take us to your father's guns." He touched the sleep pad, towering over me with his pasty self. "We should reach Caelia by nightfall."

Of course. I was on a Consulate ship—one of the three must have been far enough away from T.O. to avoid destruction. It explained why I dreamed I was flying. Somehow he thought I knew where the guns were, and he didn't know there was someone else who could fire them.

"How long have I been asleep?"

He frowned. "Two days. So you do know where Kale was taking the guns?"

"Yes," I said. I'd play along until I had a freaking clue what exactly was going on. I shrugged, trying to look non-chalant. "Generally speaking, that is. Kale took the map with him, so we need to find him first. Maybe I could do it without the map. Let me think. Kale said he was going to the moon of the planet five light-years away from the western side of Caelia, no, maybe it was the fifth moon of the planet three light-years, no, maybe it was a planet, not a moon—"

"Enough!" He slammed his hand against the wall, then grabbed a com device and barked orders to someone about needing more meds for my "attitude." He turned to me and smiled, his teeth shining like razors beneath thin lips. "Rest a little and then we'll talk more about where to find Callie."

"Excuse me?" Goose bumps rippled down my arms.

"Callie. The caller told us just today that you knew where to find Callie City." His eyes searched my face, as if the map was etched across it with an X to mark where the guns were. I'd spit at him if I had the energy to lift my head off the pillow. His voice was a low growl. "A few of the outly-ing moons and planets have had rogue cities established by those who don't appreciate the wisdom of the Consulate. I'm sure your city can be found among them."

"Sure . . . Callie City. Yep, that's where they are." I

couldn't decide whether he or Kale was the bigger asshole. My eyelids threatened to shut any second, then flung open. "Today? How did you talk to him today?"

The jerk smirked at his fellow Consulate members as he addressed me. "You haven't even asked about your companion—the one who saved you. It was a miracle he survived that explosion himself. He's sustained some kind of trauma though—he wouldn't speak after telling us about Callie City. When you're up to it, we'd like you to visit him. He's down the hall."

I closed my eyes, trying to ignore the bodies bustling about in the room. James was on board the ship. A woman lifted my arm, murmuring something about meds, then injected something in my arm. Lazy warmth flowed through my veins, and fatigue enveloped me. I quickly understood how you could get addicted to stuff like this.

My brain's processing ability grew limited as the pull of sleep intensified. So James had called the Consulate to rescue me. He'd called them before he even shot me, meaning he'd planned it all along. Did that mean he was working with the Consulate? It was hard to wrap my head around the fact that he'd shot me, yet had also saved me. I had so many questions for him, if I didn't kill him first.

Eventually I knew I'd have to come up with answers about the guns for the shiny, bespectacled man. However, my father always told me to look at the bright side, and at least I'd accomplished my goal of getting the hell off of Earth. I had no idea where my father's guns were, but I intended to find out as soon as the meds wore off.

My tenuous grip on consciousness slipped, and I drifted back into the dream realm. No matter. I'd take their drugs. I'd sleep for now. But I would wake up again. And I'd grow stronger. I'd make them sorry they ever saved my ass from that ship. I'd make them pay for my mom, my dad, and especially, Callie. I'd be worse than any burner they'd ever seen.

After checking my vital signs, I heard the last of the shiny coats leave the room. At last, I was by myself.

But I wasn't alone.

Acknowledgments

THEY SAY IT TAKES A VILLAGE TO RAISE A CHILD, AND I'D LIKE to thank the small village of people who helped me to shape this book into its final version. First, I have to thank my fabulous critique partners who saw something special in the mess that was the earliest draft of this book: Lacey J. Edwards, Valerie Kemp, Jeanne Ryan, Niki Schoenfeldt, Kelly Dyksterhouse, Joanne Zakula, and Mary Louise Sanchez. I'd also like to give a shout-out to the Department of Physics and Astronomy at the University of North Carolina, Chapel Hill, especially Dr. Gerald Cecil, for help with all things astrophysics. As I took great liberties with the information given to me, all errors of science are entirely mine.

The guidance from my rock star agent, Jessica Regel,

and my awesome editor, Greg Ferguson, was invaluable in the final stages of this book, and I'm so grateful to be working with such talented people.

A huge thanks to my parents, siblings, and friends whose encouragement helped me throughout this crazy book-writing process. Finally, this book wouldn't exist at all without the unending love and support of my amazing husband and two always-inspiring kiddos.

Follow Tora's adventures in

Chapter ONE

Three Months Later

THE BOY FACED AWAY FROM ME, LOOKING AT SOMETHING IN the distance. His profile showed off short blond hair cut in a military style, which contrasted with the stubble across his jaw. Something about him was familiar and made my heart race. I looked down to find he was holding my hand, and I felt both terrified and safe. A loud sound echoed nearby and he turned toward me. That's when I saw the gun in his hand. Fear caused my throat to tighten as his eyes locked with mine.

"Hurry, run. Come with me," he said. The inflection in his voice made the words sound like a plea.

My eyes flew open and the dream dissipated. Sweat drenched my body and my teeth chattered. I struggled to pull up the blanket but it, too, was soaked. Pain racked my head as I tried to figure out where the hell I was. Judging by the temperature, I was being held in a giant icebox.

When I attempted to sit up, my arms refused to support my weight. My eyes fell on a small device near my right hand, and I summoned all my energy to press its red button. The pounding in my head competed with widespread chills.

A high-pitched beeping of a nearby monitor permeated my consciousness. Goose bumps broke out on my arms as my skin registered the cold air. An extra thin blanket lay on the cot by my feet, yet I couldn't find the strength to pull it up. My eyes had trouble focusing, and I could just make out the gigantic form coming toward me. A mix of relief and hostility swirled through my brain. I couldn't think straight. I didn't know what it meant.

"Morning, Miss Sunshine," the large woman grumbled. "Couldn't even wait another hour for your dose, could you?"

I stared back at the red button under my finger. So I'd caused the beeping sound. The woman grabbed my arm as though she expected resistance, but my limb was limp in her hand. Her dark eyes bored into me as she lifted a green med tube and pressed the tip of it to my arm. I swear she smirked as she pressed the injection trigger.

Instant warmth flooded my veins and my body relaxed. Everything felt right with the world again. Something small nagged at the back of my mind—something I was supposed to do, or remember—but the meds quickly swept the troubled thoughts away. A familiar deep heaviness settled in and my eyelids drooped. Utter bliss and peace filled me, and I yawned as the woman retreated wordlessly from the room. I couldn't remember my own name if my life depended on it, not that it mattered. I felt great. I could stay here forever.

A deep voice echoed throughout the room as I drifted in and out of consciousness. I didn't see anyone, so maybe I was hallucinating. The voice said the same things over and over again. *The Consulate serves. The Consulate protects. The Consulate's weapons help us to protect you. The Consulate is your friend.*

Every once in a while I'd stir awake and swear someone was in the room with me. I caught the scent of wildflowers a few times, yet when I opened my eyes, the room was empty. I drifted back into sleep but couldn't shake the feeling that I wasn't really alone.

I tried to clear my thoughts, but whatever meds the woman gave me made my brain feel like mush. I remembered being injured and aboard a ship. A Consulate ship. The Consulate must have saved me from something and brought me here. Was this Caelia?

The Consulate is your friend.

I stared up at the faceless voice. The Consulate must be helping me to get better. *Then why is that woman so unpleasant? And why can't I remember anything?*

A brief scan around the windowless room provided little in the way of clues. The walls were definitely not those of a ship. The sparse furniture consisted only of the ramshackle cot I occupied and a rickety bedside table that tottered on three legs. I shifted on the bed and felt the tube between my legs. I stared in horror at the urine-filled bag that it led to. The fact that I couldn't piss on my own meant I must be really sick.

Push the button. My finger inched toward the device. Pushing the button would end the headache and icy cold. The large woman would help me. She'd give me medicine to make me feel better. My hand trembled as it touched the button, but I hesitated. Disjointed thoughts raced through my brain. Even scarier than not knowing where I was, was not knowing *who* I was.

The deep voice started in again from above. *The Consulate serves. The Consulate protects. The Consulate's weapons help us to protect you. The Consulate is your friend.* I stared at the ceiling and noticed a small device where the voice seemed to be coming from. It stopped suddenly as the sound of footsteps reached my door, followed by hushed voices. I allowed myself to slide back against the pillow and closed my eyes as the door opened. More footsteps came to the side of my bed.

"She's an hour past her dose but hasn't pushed the button. What do you think, doctor?" It was the large woman who had given me the injection of amazing medicine,

Just open your eyes and she'll give it to you. Your pain will disappear. I tried to ignore the voice in my head.

"She's still out cold and I don't want an accidental overdose. She's no good to us dead." An image of spectacles and a shiny coat popped into my head, but disappeared again. He must be one of the doctors treating my illness, whatever it was. But what did he mean by overdose?

He felt my pulse and scanned me with something that caused a warm buzzing over my body. I wanted them to leave. The doctor's hand rested on my arm and a chill went down my spine. He cleared his throat. "Are you awake?"

I pretended to stir. "Mmmm."

"It's Dr. Sorokin. How are you feeling?"

It took so much effort to form words. "I'm not sure. What's wrong with me? Where am I?"

Dr. Sorokin glanced at the woman before answering me with a question of his own. "What do you remember?"

I focused my thoughts but it was all a hazy blur. "All I remember is a Consulate ship but I don't remember why I was there. I think I was hurt. Why can't I remember anything?"

Dr. Sorokin smiled at the woman. The look on his face was smug, almost triumphant. I didn't like it. "Yes, you were injured. Sometimes trauma can cause memory loss, so I wouldn't worry too much about it. You are safe now—you're in a Consulate center on Caelia, the new Earth." He studied my face, as though waiting for a reaction. "How do you feel about the Consulate?"

I knew the word *Consulate* meant something to me, but all I could recall was what I'd heard from the ceiling. I struggled to speak again. "Are they the ones who gave me these meds?"

Dr. Sorokin's hand was icy on my arm. I wanted to pull away but didn't have the strength. "Yes, the Consulate is giving you medicine to help you get better."

I started to drift off again but fought it. "Then I think they're fabulous. I love the Consulate." My eyes fluttered shut, and I hoped they'd think I had fallen back asleep. All I wanted was this man to take his cold hand off my body.

He shook my arm but I played dead. Dr. Sorokin sighed and spoke to the woman. "Give her two more hours, max, then wake her. Allan thinks we can safely begin Phase Two. We started too early last time. These drugs should have erased a lot of her memories by now, and she's so dependent on them that she'll do whatever we want to get more. We have her just where we want her."

The woman chuckled. "Heard her mother was an addict too. Guess we don't need to worry about this one running away again."

They left the room. My brain tried—and failed—to compute what I'd just heard. I had run away from these people? That meant I was a prisoner. I could barely manage to push a button, yet somehow I had attempted to escape this place. And they'd said I was dependent on drugs. That explained why I craved the meds so badly. But the woman's comment stuck with me. She'd said my mother was an addict too. *Mother? Where was my mother?*

I fought off sleep as another wave of exhaustion crashed into me. Whatever Dr. Sorokin had in store for me wasn't good—I knew that much. The haze started to confuse my brain again, but I pushed through the fog to search for memories. Fractured images swirled, then slowly merged in my mind. Images of a fiery red sun, an army of guns, a boy with blond stubble and a sandpaper voice, a father bent over a notebook, and last, a little girl in a pale flowered shirt. My eyes widened in shock as the pictures crystallized. It took all of my strength to lift my hand and wipe the beads of sweat from my forehead. I opened my mouth and my voice was still weak and scratchy, but I heard myself clearly.

"I am Tora Reynolds."

Though I had no clue how long I'd been held captive, all that mattered was the two short hours I had left before Dr. Sorokin and Nurse Nasty came back for me. It was still hard to comprehend that after refusing meds my entire life, I'd become an even worse addict than my mother. Against my will but an addict nonetheless.

A fresh batch of sweat poured from my skin, and the

throbbing in my head resumed. Was it more sad or funny that though I wanted to escape, I couldn't help but feel that a "tiny dose" of meds would help the process go more smoothly?

I surveyed my attire and sighed. The only thing on me was a thermoplastic gown, presumably for easier access to the catheter tubing. That would have to go first. I took a deep breath and pulled out the long, thin tube. I winced as it slid out, and mentally filed the task under "Things I Never Want to Do Again."

Then I leaned over and checked the drawer in the bed-side table, but it was empty. I had a vague recollection of my satchel but it was nowhere in sight. Guess I'd have to make do with the gown. Not that I had much chance of blending in, anyway, with my shaking hands and sweat-drenched hair. The door seemed incredibly far away as I swung my legs to the floor.

I took an unsteady step and had to lean on the table for support. I tried again and made it two whole steps before my knees buckled and I fell. It was like I was learning to walk all over again. My fingers brushed the cold tile and I inhaled deeply. *You can do this,* I told myself. *Yeah, but wouldn't it be easier with a little help of the chemical variety?* I gritted my teeth. At this rate it would take the whole two hours just to make it to the door. I pushed up from the floor. After what felt like a million shaky steps, I reached it and leaned my head against the cold surface.

No footsteps sounded outside, so I reached for the door handle with bated breath. There was no energetic lock that I could see. It was open. Guess being in a vegetative state for so long had lulled these people into a false sense of security. Good thing, because if it had been locked, I think I would have laid down right there and taken a nap.

The door opened easily, but it still took a crazy amount of effort on my part. How in the hell was I going to escape if opening a door was problematic? The hallway was clear, but I had no idea which way to go. It wasn't like they had the flashing exit signs that had lined the halls of Dad's Consulate building job. Dad's Consulate job. A whole new host of memories flooded back, and I pushed them away for the time being. I needed to get out of this place first.

My room was around the center point of the hallway, and it stretched about thirty feet on either side. There were no windows. One direction looked to be a few feet shorter than the other, so I headed that way. It was just as cold in the hall as in my room. Only a few dim lights hung from makeshift holders on the wall.

The entire building looked primitive in construction, consisting of a dark brown material I'd never seen before. Still, it was an actual building, which meant I'd probably been here awhile. It had to have been several months since I'd been picked up by the Consulate ship. Several months since I'd tried to keep my dad's bioenergetic weapons out of enemy hands and failed miserably. Guns that only I—and apparently James—could fire. Several months since Kale had landed on that crazy-ass shifting planet, watched James shoot me, and then took off with the guns when the Consulate descended. I saw the lasers from the soldiers' guns tear into James right before I'd detonated T.O., the most powerful bomb ever made.

James. The name sent shivers down my spine. When the shivers increased to the point of shaking, I realized that withdrawal, rather than conflicted feelings, was the culprit. My limbs twitched uncontrollably, and I broke out in a sweat yet again. The urge to vomit was overwhelming.

It was impossible that my skin felt so hot, but I was so cold, like an icy fire ran through my veins instead of blood. *Ticktock.* I'd killed at least thirty minutes already and was getting nowhere fast. My long-term plan of finding Kale and the guns was toast if my short-term goal of walking didn't go so well. I pushed myself to take several more steps. There were no other doors in this hallway. I made it to the corner and turned. This corridor was shorter, only about twenty feet long and ended at a door.

About fifteen feet away from me on the right was another door, but it was the end of the hallway that made my heart skip. Faint light shone from behind it. It had to be an exit. I hobbled along as quickly as possible. The cold feeling had entirely disappeared. In fact, it felt downright toasty. Maybe this was a lull in the withdrawal symptoms.

I hoped so because I'd sweated out most of the liquid in my body and would kill for some Caelia Pure.

I'd gotten about halfway down the hall when I heard a noise from somewhere behind me. I turned around but saw nothing there. As I took another step, other sounds became clearer—footsteps and voices. It was the large woman and someone else. Not the doctor, but the person sounded vaguely familiar.

They had to be heading toward my room. The sound of a door opening followed by the woman's loud, panicked voice confirmed it. No way had it been two hours, had it? Crap. I attempted to run to the exit, but it ended up being more like a drunken shuffle. I'd never make it.

The door on my right-hand side was only a foot away. It didn't have a lock either and was my only shot. They would turn the corner in a second and see me. I lurched for the door. Inside, I shut it and pressed my back against it to keep them out. My legs were rubbery and I knew I couldn't hold on for much longer. I was out of juice.

I leaned my head back and looked around the room. It was identical to mine, down to the bed and table. Down to a figure lying comatose in the center of the bed, though the person, at least, had managed to pull the covers up around him. Curious about my fellow prisoner, I stepped toward the bed. It wasn't like I had the strength to keep anyone out of the room anyway.

The blanket covered most of his face, but his forehead

was covered in sweat. At least I assumed it was a "he" due to the short gray hair. It must be close to his next dose time too. The building's cooling system must have been out of whack—unless they were using a bizarre method of torture by climate control. I reached out and tugged the cover down. *Holy mother of god.*

I couldn't even comprehend what I was seeing. Maybe it was a hallucination from the drugs. His eyes widened in shock and confusion that must have mirrored my own.

"Tora? Is that you?" his voice croaked.

I touched his face to make sure it was real.

"Yes. Yes, Dad. It's me."

Chapter TWO

DAD REACHED FOR MY WRIST AND ATTEMPTED TO SIT UP. HIS hand was frail and bony. I helped pull him to a seated position and placed a pillow behind him so he could lean back. He struggled to speak. "They told me you were dead. All this time, I thought you were dead."

I squeezed his hand. "They told me the same thing about you." The fact that he sat here in front of me still wasn't totally registering. I think it was a combination of shock and the drugs.

His sunken eyes were so different from the calm, confident gaze I remembered. He'd glance up from his notebooks to wave me into his study, and I'd curl up to read on the bench in his room while he worked, always feeling safe when he was near. Now, he didn't look like he could protect himself, let alone anyone else. "What have they done to you, Dad? Have they had you all this time?"

"Ever since that so-called meeting back on Earth. I should have known it was a trap. They said they'd let me go as soon as I told them where the guns were. Later, they claimed they'd found the guns and that you were dead, so I might as well work with them." His voice broke. "I still wouldn't cooperate, so after they transported me to Caelia, they started experimenting with various drugs. Drugs to make me compliant." He coughed. "I guess I'm still not very compliant, though."

"Like father, like daughter." I patted his arm. "They gave me different drugs too. Ones to make me forget. They thought if I lost my memories, I'd forget what burners they were."

I remembered the last page of Mom's journal, the one where Dad had written about how I'd locked Callie out of the bunker. How Callie had died and then Mom sank next to her by the boulder and let herself burn alive right outside our shelter door. A torrent of emotions overcame me. Guilt. Grief. Relief.

The reality of Dad being alive finally hit me, and I threw my arms around him. All those lonely nights after he never returned from that meeting when I thought he'd been killed. A sob tore from my throat. "I'm so sorry about Mom and Callie," I said. "I read the journal. I never meant—"

"Shhh," said Dad. "That's not important now. What

matters is that you're okay." Tears leaked from his eyes. "I can't believe you're sitting here in front of me."

"We can't stay here long. They'll find us. We need to get you out of here." I glanced around the room and back at Dad, who didn't look strong enough to walk ten feet. Not that I was in much better shape.

The reunion was short-lived. The door flew open, banging against the wall. I stared openmouthed at the person standing next to the woman. Alec. The guy from Sector 2 who I'd talked Markus into rescuing back on Earth. How was this possible? The heavyset woman gasped for air, red-faced as she bent over with her hand to her chest. I might have a slight chance in hell of getting by her, but I'd never get by Alec.

Alec stared at me calmly as he spoke. "Tora Reynolds, you have violated Consulate Code 5223 by attempting to leave the premises."

I wanted to kick myself for ever buying his act about being an abandoned survivor, though the dog thing was a nice touch. Where was Lucy? I should have saved the dog and left him to rot.

"Really? Is there a code for kidnapping and drugging innocent people, 'cause I'm pretty sure you're in violation of that one." I no longer considered his accent cute. My legs wobbled underneath me, and I had to sit on the edge of Dad's bed.

The large woman finally found her breath, along

with her evil smile. "I believe you know Lieutenant Colonel Alec Hayes. He was instrumental in helping us to locate you on Earth."

If I'd had an ounce of strength left, I would've launched myself at him and torn his eyes out. Instead, I glared with all the venom I could muster, which probably looked plain pitiful given my current condition. "You freakin' burner."

Alec stared back without bothering to respond. The woman pulled a syringe from her pocket and handed it to him. "You can do the honors."

She smirked at me. "You will never, ever run away again. I'll see to that." Spit flew from her mouth and I pretended to wipe my cheek.

Alec came toward me and spun the syringe in his hand like he was playing with it. He wasn't just following orders—he seemed to be enjoying himself. I hoped he injected himself by accident.

I let loose a string of every expletive I could think of but my words were hollow, and I couldn't back them up with action. My legs were done. They felt like jelly against the bed.

"Please don't do this." Dad put his hand up weakly in Alec's direction. "I'll do whatever you want, but don't hurt Tora."

The woman's lips curled back, revealing yellowed teeth. "You promised that before, remember? You don't follow through so well."

Alec reached my side.

"It's okay, Dad." I gave his arm an awkward hug. "I've made it this far. I'll get you out of here, I promise."

The woman laughed. "Over my dead body."

I shrugged at her. "Have it your way."

Alec pulled my arm out roughly. Tears pricked my eyes. Why was he doing this? He placed the syringe against the place where my bicep muscle used to be and pressed the button.

Everything swam before my eyes and then went dark. As I hit the floor, it dawned on me that though Alec had been holding my arm, he didn't even try to break my fall.

James sat next to me on a cot. I looked past him toward the door. We were in my room in the containment center, and I knew we had to be careful. Someone wanted to hurt us. His hazel-green eyes stared into mine. "Please," he said, then his lips were on mine. My body responded though my brain screamed for me to stop. His hands moved slowly down my arms. Then he tightened his grip. I tried to pull away, but he wouldn't let go. He started shaking me.

I gradually came out of the dream but couldn't fully wake. The shaking didn't stop. It wasn't just my arms. My entire body quaked. Great. *More withdrawal symptoms.* I didn't want to open my eyes. Maybe I could sleep through it. I tried to slip back into unconsciousness. The spasms continued.

From a faraway place, someone called my name. Finally, I realized that I wasn't shaking—someone was shaking me.

I fought the urge to wake up.

"Dammit, open your eyes!"

He didn't have to be so rude about it. It took tremendous effort, but my eyelids cracked open to slits. "What? I'm trying to sleep here," I mumbled. My eyes crashed shut again.

Cold water sprayed my face and my eyes flew open. *Alec.* I swung my fist at him but he easily caught my hand. "Knock it off, Tora. We have to go."

I blinked. "I'm not going anywhere with you."

Alec sighed as though I was acting like a petulant child. "I didn't give you the dose. I switched the syringe with another one I had in my pocket." He pulled on my arm.

I twisted out of his grasp with what little strength I had. "Do you think I'm stupid? If you didn't give me the dose, then why have I slept like the dead for hours?"

He pulled out a pair of cotton pants and a T-shirt from a bag. "Not hours, *ángel.* Minutes. I gave you a quick-acting sleep agent, but had to make it look real." He tossed the clothes at me. "We don't have much time before Sylvia comes back."

"You must be referring to the big-boned bee-atch."

Alec nodded. "There's a med to help with the withdrawal symptoms, but Sylvia must have moved it. I didn't have time to keep looking."

I fingered the pants and frowned. "Wait, these are *my* pants."

"Yes, from your things in storage." He gestured for me to hurry.

Something about having my own pants made me insanely happy. I picked up the white T-shirt. "But this isn't mine . . . it's way too big—" No way. I held the shirt to my nose and inhaled. The scent of him was faint, but still there. *Because what could be more romantic than wearing the shirt of the guy who shot you?*

Now Alec looked impatient. "I don't know what to tell you, but it was with your stuff. Can we please leave now?" He tossed me my satchel with the rest of my things. Callie's wildflower painting was there. I resisted the urge to pull it out and nodded at him.

Alec waited outside while I changed. The T-shirt hung loosely over my pants—I had to admit it was comfy. My legs were still weak, but the thought of getting out of this place propelled me to the door.

Alec glanced down the hallway and motioned me forward.

I sniffed. "Just because I'm coming with you doesn't mean you don't have a lot of explaining to do."

He placed his hand under my elbow to support me. "Don't worry. We'll have plenty of time for that."

Dad's door was just ahead. He was in much worse shape than I was—probably because he'd been imprisoned longer. I hoped he could at least walk. I slowed as we neared his room.

Alec shook his head. "Tora—"

"I'm not leaving without him." I opened the door to an empty room. The cot was stripped bare, no evidence that it had ever been occupied by my only living family member. I swiveled to face Alec. "Where is he?"

He tugged on my arm to pull me toward the exit. "He's fine. They moved him somewhere else. They didn't want to chance another escape attempt. They figured you'd try to take him with you."

I pulled my arm back. "Then we need to find him."

Alec sighed. "We will, but not now. I don't know exactly where he is, but I do know that we're almost out of time. We'll come back, but you can't help your dad if you're caught again."

Alec had a point. I watched him pull a small metal object from his shirt when we reached the final door.

"What is that?"

"It's a key from an old-school lock on Earth. The Consulate brought a bunch of this stuff from the archives building to hold them over until they got their technology up and running."

I thought of my dad's high-tech guns and wondered if they were still in Kale's possession. Alec slid the key into the lock on the door and turned it. "I think they had a bit of a shock coming here. They had all the Earth money they could ever want, which didn't mean anything once they landed. Everyone went back to survival mode."

The door opened and Alec stepped outside. "Wait!" I shrieked. "Don't we need suits?"

Alec put his finger to his lips to shush me but showed a hint of a smile. "Nope. There's plenty of air on Caelia, and the sun is, well, it's different. Come on."

I took a hesitant step out into the daylight. The sun was a gold color, much smaller than the huge red inferno that had ruled Earth. I stretched out my bare arm and the sunlight warmed my skin. Memories of blisters popping out on my hands, of Mom and Callie burning alive, reared up to haunt me. I tried in vain to pull my short sleeves down for cover. "My arm. It feels hot."

Alec grabbed my arm and urged me onward. "You're fine. It's not going to burn. Have I mentioned we need to get out of here?"

I willed my legs to cooperate, but their plans favored sitting and resting. I hung on to Alec and stared down at my legs as though I could make them remain upright with the power of my gaze.

"Come on, hurry," Alec said. "We just need to make it to the tree line."

"The tree what?" I looked up from my feet and gasped. Trees. Real trees as far as the eye could see. We were in a clearing in the midst of a ton of huge, leafy, green trees. It was a far cry from the deadly, sharp cactus groves on

Earth. I struggled to recall the word I'd seen on my Infinity and gestured at the friendly-looking foliage. "What's this called again?"

Alec smiled but didn't stop tugging at me. "It's a forest."

I tried it out. "Forest." The word sounded beautiful on my tongue. "It's my new favorite word."

"I think there's a word you'll like even better, but we'll never get there if the Consulate catches us."

As though on cue, loud shouts echoed from inside the building we'd escaped. "Guess Sylvia just figured out I'm missing . . . again," I said.

My legs churned sluggishly beneath me, but I was determined to get to the forest. It killed me that I had to leave my dad so soon after discovering he wasn't dead. *Sorry, Dad,* I thought. *I'll be back for you as soon as I can.* I would get him out of there somehow, and the Consulate was going to pay for what they'd done to him.

Alec didn't let go of my arm. My feet tripped over themselves as I tried to keep up.

We hit the tree line just as the building door opened. Alec pulled me behind a large tree and we looked into the clearing. Sylvia was bent at the knees and looked as though she was about to throw up. Next to her was the shiny-coated, fake-glasses-wearing Dr. Sorokin, who had treated me on the Consulate ship. He turned around in a slow circle, peering into the trees that surrounded the building.

I stared at the ugly, bleak building in the center of the lush forest. They'd obviously cut down some of the trees to make room for their makeshift prison. Leave it to the Consulate—they'd found an amazing, beautiful planet and had already started to wreck it.

After a minute, Dr. Sorokin reached into his pocket and pulled out a tele-com device.

Alec tugged at my sleeve. "He's calling for Consulate backup. We have to go," he whispered.

Cold sweats, fatigue, and nausea warred for control of my body. Though another visit with the shiny coats was the last thing I wanted, I was pretty positive I couldn't move another step.

"Where are we going?" I asked, swaying.

Alec's eyes bored into mine as he steadied me. "Somewhere I know you'll want to see. Callie City."